at the Dusk of Madness

at the Dusk of Madness

Joshua Bunnell

I want to dedicate this book to my close family. During the stretched years I was writing these tales it was their words of encouragement and support that drove me to publish my first book.

To My wife -- Christen, I'm indebted to you for your unwavering support towards my publishing dreams.

To my children -- Jeremiah and Kiya, your excitement and pride you show me with every book I publish affects me beyond anything mere words can express.

To my parents -- Phil and Lacey, the way you raised me encouraged my imagination to mature into what others are reading now.

To my sister -- Samantha, we may not see eye to eye on many topics (which include a good many authors and books), but through it all you encourage me from a far. Though there are a few stories in this volume I know you've said are not your favorite, I genuinely accept and appreciate your honesty.

To my grandmother -- Marcelline, though she's long departed. I know she'd be proud of what I've accomplished.

**Books by
Joshua Bunnell**

at the Dusk of Madness

<u>Coming Soon</u>

Dark Happenings . . . in the land of the mundane
A Soul Damns The Soul
Cody / McIntire Mysteries (OMNIBUS)

Contents

at the Dusk of Madness

From an infectious mind, I could not find.
     Any way to remain blind,
to the tales of macabre redefined.
Then to jot them down intertwined,
and on the white-lined paper bind.
– I can do nothing more refined,
locking in place the psychosis and the divine.
These voices have boldness,
who tell me tales of cruel darkness.
I am but a canvas,
to bring light to their crassness.
I do not hold tight the harness,
to these creatures who lack kindness.
I'm afraid in great sadness.
I'm at the dusk of madness.

The Damned Rain

"Joseph McAllister step forward," orders a giant of a man from behind a desk of solid white marble.

"That's me, sir," replies an average looking man with mid-length hair and a scruffy face. He sticks out from the surrounding environment, due to the simplistic fact everything else is white, while he wears a gray jogging suit with green stripes. Even the giant behind the desk wears a white shroud. The man looks around in wonder to find no one else.

"Are you aware as to what has happened to you?" asks the giant as he looks to Joseph.

"Not really," he quietly replies. With this answer the giant flips the great book before him open.

"Joseph McAllister you are dead. You have been in limbo for what you'd call eight months, while your life was reviewed to determine you eternal residence," he explains.

"Wow, eight months. I guess the correctional system is slow no matter where you go," Joseph comments with a chuckle. The giant upon hearing his levity slams his closed fist upon the marble filling the white space with a sound that can only be described as a tremendous thunderclap. Joseph's attention is instantly redirected by this violent action.

"This is no laughing matter!" yells the giant in a booming voice.

"I'm sorry, what do you mean?" he asks in a softer voice then before.

"It is a record of what you'd call your pathetic existence," he responds.

"So where am I now?" he asks.

"You are in the Court of Morality. I am known by many names, but you may call me Yanluo Wang, overseer of judgment of souls and decider as to their eternal placement. You are here because of certain issues surrounding your death. However, you are also here to plea your justification on this life you lead of grave misdeeds," answers Yanluo. "Are you fully understanding of your situation? So we may begin your inquest?"

"Yes," he answers back solemnly.

"Good, I've got fifteen thousand to review and they are never-ending," comments Yanluo. He flips to the front of Joseph's book. "At the age of five, you pushed and struck nearly two dozen of your peers. The total number of physical assaults committed at this age stops at twenty-three. How do you argue these facts?" questions Yanluo.

"Huh?" Joseph says, forcing a short pause of shocked surprise. "I was five years old. I mean I was a little kid."

"You were morally of age to know the difference of right and wrong," he argues back to the dumbfounded man.

"But what does that have to do with the latter part of my life?" Joseph counters. "Everyone misbehaves when they're young, that's the whole point. To screw-up and learn from it."

"That's the gravity of these earlier transgressions. You never did learn from them and they worsened as you grew ever older," retorts Yanluo. "When you were fourteen, this was a big time of growth for you. We'll skip the lesser marks and focus on the big ones." Joseph shifts his feet in his telling sign of nervousness. "You committed, with assistance, thirteen robberies within this year. You followed up by committing your first act of rape, which you continued to commit regularly for the remaining course of your wicked life. Do you wish to refute any of these charges?"

"Would there be any point?" asks Joseph with a brisk scoff.

"No," Yanluo replies. Joseph doesn't speak, simply shakes his head in reply to the previous question directed to him.

"Very well. Let's move on to when you were twenty-three. This one is filled by twenty-seven robberies, nineteen acts of violent rape, and a pyramid scheme where you stole fifty thousand dollars from poor old ladies. That was quite a proud year for you. The next twenty-two years follows in much the same way," he states. This is followed with a pause to see if Joseph wishes to make any comments. Joseph stands before the marble table and makes not a sound. Yanluo once more continues the inquest of Joseph McAllister.

"This inquest has nearly reached a verdict, but there are a few remaining issues to cover," explains Yanluo. "The first is a discrepancy within the merits of your death. You died, while shoving a middle-aged woman out of oncoming traffic. In turn, out of this action the semi-truck struck, killing you, not her. This last act of self-sacrifice counters your lifetime of misdeeds. This action qualifies you to enter the gates into the kingdom of the heavenly hereafter. The question has been raised if there may have been another reason as to why you committed such a selfless act? While you've been here, I have taken the liberty to search your thoughts for this very answer and found one I have."

"You cannot do that!" exclaims Joseph with worry filling his face. Yanluo does not speak. He simply bangs his closed fist once more on the marble table, silencing Joseph's outburst.

"Upon searching your thoughts I've recalled said memory. In it I have found the true reason you saved her life," says Yanluo. "You were running from a couple of shady men whom you owed a long overdue debt. You did not see her or the semi before accidentally bumping into her knocking her from off the path of the barreling semi-truck. Therefore, my ruling on this incident is not one of self-sacrifice, but of self-preservation. You have no concern for any life, but that of your own. You ended your existence as you lived it, selfishly. At this time do you have anything further to add before placement is set?" On this final address to the condemned soul Yanluo goes silent in quiet wait for him say his peace.

"You pass judgment over me! Yet you've not lived how I have lived. I have lived helpless, homeless, alone, treated by others with malice, and I have been an outcast my whole life. Forcefully, denied even the slightest ounce of society's happiness. You call my actions misdeeds? I call them survival. Pass your verdict. I don't care anymore. There, that's my final plea. Now let's get on with it," Joseph passionately replies. He waits in a silent stare as Yanluo enters Joseph's final speech into the book. Joseph knows whatever decision is made he'll deal with it as he's dealt with life.

"It is the verdict of the Court of Morality that you -- Joseph McAllister -- are to be sentenced to an eternity of helping the very life from, which you've taken so very much. You're spiritual entity shall be transformed into fifty thousand raindrops. Your sole purpose will be to bring life to the lifeless, give hope where hope is lost, and give endlessly without ever taking for yourself. This shall be your eternal penance for a life of selfishness and greed. Now, be gone Joseph McAllister!" orders Yanluo as he sends the man from the room with a wave of his mighty hand.

Directly following Joseph's eternal verdict many astral planes away from the Court of Morality. In a small farm town in the middle of Kansas a rain begins to fall from a cloud seemingly appearing from out of thin air. The rain starts out slow at first, but gradually picks up until the sky is filled with clear drops of liquid life ending the worst drought in the state's history for two decades.

Unseen Voices

"**M**ark, are you sure you don't have any more questions for me before I leave?" asks the old man, who's working the morning shift at the full-service gas station.

"I'm sure, Mort, I've already asked all the questions I've had during my training," replies Mark as he's anxiously waits to start his first solo shift.

"I'm sure you'll be fine. Besides, Sunday night tends to be one of the slowest shifts of the week," adds Mort. With this parting comfort the older man grabs his lunch cooler and waddles to his old red truck. Once inside he tries turning over the engine. Luckily, by the third try it finally rolls over with only a slight amount of fuss. Before Mort departs he leaves a haze from two smoking backfires coming out of the truck's twin mufflers. Mark is promptly visited by three passing patrons each purchase varies in their quantity of fuel. After a couple of hours of business the surge of customers grinds to a horrifying halt.

Mark sits beside pump five in a fold-out camping chair staring along the motionless road lying ahead of him. Dusk closes in with his attention transfixed into complete boredom. Something jerks him from his untimely slumber, a voice, a very sad echo of a young woman. The voice comes from over his left shoulder and in reflex he jumps to look. Even though he knows there is no one near the station by a couple miles. After his search is satisfied he settles back into the chair. It's not long before he hears the voice again. This time he feels a set of ice cold fingers rest upon his shoulder. Unlike before the saddened voice yells directly behind his left ear. The sheer volume of the voice causes him to jolt forward in reflex resulting with him falling face first to the hard ground. In frightened terror he looks everywhere. He moves, looking around the two four-pump islands forming the station's commerce.

The next day, the young man comes into the station around noon. Mort and a younger old man stand watch over the pumps. After Mark parks his car to the far backside of the parking lot he walks over to his fellow attendants.

"So how was last night?" asks Mort on Mark reaching the pump station.

"Everything went fine enough," he answers. "I know you're going to think I'm crazy, but I was sitting on that chair when I heard a faint voice. Later I heard the voice again, but the second time it sounded like she was yelling in my ear and touched my shoulder." He looks to his coworkers, while nervously handing the bank bag with the night's earnings to Mort.

"It was probably just an echo. Assuming no one was 'round?" asks the younger yet older man who's nicknamed "Motor", since he's always got something to say. "Yeah herd an echo, we'ra in a valley and the mountain ova looks us on three sides. So echoes carry for a while hea," Motor finishes explaining. Mark simply nods in understanding even though he knows damn well it was no echo. He's pulled to the side by Mort away from Motor.

"Look. The first night on shift alone can be scary, especially when no one is around to help. Like you told me the other day you grew up in New York and you only recently moved out here to the sticks. I'm sure being here must be like night to your New York days. I've lived here all my life so I'm used to the unnatural quiet of the woods. I guess for someone like you who are used to the hustle and bustle of the big city it can seem overwhelming," Mort tries in vain to comfort Mark's spooked stare.

"Thanks, Mort," he replies.

"Besides you can recollect your wits. You have the next three days off, my boy," adds Mort. After the proper exchange of pleasantries Mark walks across the dust-covered parking lot to his car he returns home to his well-bosomed new bride and his precious newborn daughter Emma.

After three days basking in his new family's glow he returns to the gas station for his second solo night shift.

"Well, I'm outta hea Maak. Now rememba if'n that ghost shows up again tell ha we can't honoa ha checks," jokes Motor. He walks to his black Thunderbird. Unlike Mort's, Motor's fires up on the first try followed by his wheels kicking up a world of dust and rock as he floors it out of the parking lot. The night ventures on like the previous where the bustle of people slows as dusk creeps in from the east. This time he has made sure not to become even the slightest bit groggy. His inner voice had suggested over the last three days that maybe this is what triggered the voice. It's around seven-thirty and the end of the shift is three hours off. The last customer he had was at six thirty-five.

"How can this place make any money with this kind of business?" he asks out loud to himself. While pondering his own line of inquiry he suddenly feels icy fingers rest upon his shoulder. Now on first instinct he wants to turn around, but he figures that Motor snuck back to get another laugh in.

"Very funny, Motor!" he comments in a bemused voice. He turns to look to sees no one there. He rises to his feet and in one solemn movement searches behind the attendant's metal makeshift building. That is when he hears the voice again.

"Help me, please, help me," the ghostly weak voice cries out followed by what he later describes as if she's gurgling water after she spoke. He hears a great splash from the cement dugout hole, which is where the four fuel holding tanks are housed. Jumping to his feet with a flashlight in hand he races across the parking lot to the entrance of the fenced-in holding tanks. The square cement ditch is twelve feet deep. There is only a small wooden platform, which covers less than a quarter of the ditch. After searching every water-flooded section positioned between the rusty tanks he returns to his chair. *That wasn't an echo by any stretch of the imagination,* he tells himself. *It sounded so real, but there was no one there. Not even a ripple on the water's surface. It's filled with four feet of water. If anyone or anything fell in the water it would have showed signs of being disrupted.* After his fast-paced heart slows back to normal he starts his end of shift chores and paperwork. Not another sound is heard for the remainder of the night.

Since that night, which ended at the cement ditch housing the holding tanks he hasn't felt nor heard a sound. In fact, it's been two weeks since that terrifying night. Motor arrives ten minutes before his shift starts at three and Mark is finishing up the last loose ends before his shift is finished.

"Aboot dune?" Motor asks with no regards to even try to control his Down East accent.

"I'm almost done, just have to total my earnings for the shift," Mark replies. Without giving him a second glance Motor parks his cheeks on the camping chair. "Yes, dead even."

"What waz that, Maak?" asks Motor without turning his head.

"Nothing, I'm off, the stations yours, Mister Motor," farewells Mark. He runs to his car on a quick step to escape the downpouring rain. This storm has been holding on for three days and everyone hopes it lets up sooner rather than later.

After a pleasant evening with the family and a reasonable enough workday, Mark decides he deserves a restful night's sleep. Well, the best amount of sleep a parent can get with a rowdy newborn. The second his head hits the pillow he's out like a light. It annoys his wife at how easy it is for him to fall asleep, while it takes her sometimes hours of lying in their irritatingly taunting bed listening to Mark's heavy breathing.

It's one-thirty in the morning when he's woken directly from his deep sleep. Lying perfectly still on his back he listens to the metal pings of rain as they bounce off the tin-plated roof covering their elderly trailer. No matter how hard he tries to shut his eyes in the hopes of falling back asleep he can't. It's though something is forcing him to stay awake for some unknown reason. He fills with an uncontrollable need to hurry out to the gas station and more specifically the holding tanks. He tries to fight the need, but finally after five agonizing minutes he cracks. Quickly getting dressed he grabs his keys from the ceramic bowl sitting to the right side of his dresser.

"Where are you going at this time of night?" asks his exhausted wife who's had to take care of Emma five times already.

"I have to run to the station. I'll explain later, but right now I really need to hurry," he answers even though he knows she's already fallen back to sleep.

He races down the flooded roads at top speed as though his life will expire if he does not reach the station in a designated timeframe. The need to arrive is at its greatest desire when he's less than five minutes from the entrance. Rolling passed the pumps he stops to the left of the tanks. Forcing the car into park with a violent jolt he opens the driver's door to hurry to the fenced-in ditch leaving it wide open. Passing through the wire meshed fence's access door he looks into the ever filling cavity of formed cement. The ditch is now half full of water thanks mostly to the three days and nights of continuous rainfall. Looking over the water he sees nothing other than trash floating on its surface. From over his head in a split second comes a flash of lightning illuminating the ditch to allow him just enough time to spot a purple t-shirt with white flowers floating just under the surface of the water directly below. Without thinking he jumps feet first into the flooded ditch. Upon nearing the purple shirt he finds a young woman floating face down in the water half naked. After several minutes of struggling he somehow manages to lift her lifeless body out and onto the walkway above. Not knowing what to do he tries CPR after first removing the water from out of her lungs. After ten minutes of repetition she violently inhales at the surrounding air and opens her eyes. The balls of sight fix firmly on Mark, who's looking down on her. Following this relieved development he calls both an ambulance and the sheriff department. Once he's able to get her up and on her feet he helps her to sit on the front passenger seat, while they wait for help to arrive.

Within ten minutes both emergency vehicles arrive at the station. The paramedics load her into the ambulance and speed with sirens wailing back to the county hospital. With the ambulance gone the sheriff rests his attention on Mark.

"They say she'll be fine. It's a good thing you happened upon her when you did. I'm going to need you to come down to the station to fill out a statement," the sheriff asks in an order. The sheriff studies Mark's every twitch. He looks the part of a stereotypical sheriff you'd see on TV. He's in his late forties with a thick brown handle bar mustache.

"Fine. No problem," Mark answers with a short pause. "Do you know who she is?"

"We do, her name is Betsy Swan. She went missing six months back. What the medics said prior to leaving is that she's been pretty abused. It's not hard to figure out why she was tossed face down into a flooded ditch. Since she's still alive and being this is a small town I'm fairly confident we'll be able to catch the sick bastard responsible."

"It's terrible to think so many people can hurt and abuse others without so much as a glimmer of guilt," Mark comments with a tone of saddened disgust.

"Follow me to the office and we'll get your statement put down," the sheriff says. Mark nods in agreement. Both men load into their vehicles. The sheriff follows behind Mark's course in the same direction as the ambulance did, heading back to town.

Planet of Hopeful Madness

The year was 2020. A global shift caused numerous natural and man-assisted disasters to engulf our world. Only natural mass hysteria soon followed. In the end only a quarter of the globe's population survived. Those of us unlucky enough to survive the beginning storms were forced to witness a nightmarish reality. The natural carnage caused the exposure and leakage of highly toxic materials allowing the skies to fill with clouds of ash and flammable gases. One day these skies ignited into sweeping waves of atmospheric flames. Mankind's need for survival urged the once war-torn nations of the world to put aside petty disputes to form a global collective with one singular purpose. Search beyond the ash-filled skies for a new planet before time ran out.

The year is now 2045. The great minds who will lead us to salvation have broken the problem limiting the capabilities of the warp drive device. They have located four distant plants habitable in sustaining human life. These once unreachable stars are now plausible. Four scouting vessels are to be sent from Earth to check these distant stars. In order to foresee any dangers lingering beyond what preliminary scans can see along with making friends with any local inhabitants who may already call the planet home.

This is where my story begins. My name is George Cromwell, astronaut and Good Will Ambassador of Earth. My mission is to scout the distant star codenamed *Novae*. A name taken from the plural of nova, meaning a star, which suddenly increases its light output tremendously before fading away to its former obscurity in a few months or years. It's a fitting name considering, for now, it's one of our shining beacons of hope. After reaching the planet its light could fade back into the blanket of space or better still it could shine on for generations to come.

1.

"They are ready for you, George," says a short, but well-buffed man. "The preflight check list has just finished."

"Alright, Frank I'm coming," I reply. The gray jumpsuit for the mission rides up in all the wrong places. We walk down along the corridor to the shuttle car set to take us to the waiting vessel. Frank breaks into hysterics. Turning I see him lying on his back across the gray cement floor rolling in laughter with tears pouring down his cheeks and onto his oversized orange jumpsuit.

"What's so funny, you idiot?" I ask with a chuckle. With his spasm contained he returns to his feet. Facing me he sets his large hand on my left shoulder.

"Here you are one of the world's last great hopes walking down the hallway constantly pulling at the crack of your ass. It's hysterical," he explains followed by a further burst of laughter.

"The eggheads can make a warp drive rocket, but they can't tailor a comfortable jumpsuit," I reply with a returning chuckle. "Not everyone can have a suit that was made for a fat guy. What did you do trade him a donut for that suit? You can fit into it three times over."

"Actually, a whole box, thank you very much," he corrects. We continue our course down the hall. Never will I ever understand this. They have a shuttle car so we won't have to walk all the way to the ship, but we have to march down a mile and a half hallway to get to the damn vehicle? Finally reaching the car we shuttle down the runway towards Icarus Twelve.

The single passenger vessel at first glance resembles a stealth bomber only at five times the thickness. Frank and his two flunkies help secure me into my seat and take a final look around to make sure everything is tightly secured. Frank hands over my earpiece, which I place into my ear. I hear the control room calling for a COM check.

"This is Cromwell, are you hearing me, Control?" I say into the microphone positioned two inches from my lips.

"We can hear you, Cromwell. There has been a slight change in departure," says a voice into my ear.

"Change?" I ask as butterflies hatch into the base of my stomach.

"You will be glided to the appropriate altitude and detached. From there you will continue to ascend until you break Earth's atmosphere, then our orbit. From there you will proceed according to the mission directives," explains the voice.

"Understand, Control," I reply.

"We're secured, Control," reports Frank into his walkie. "Yes Control, we're proceeding to seal the cockpit's outer door." He nods for everyone to step out of the cockpit. Frank leans down by my ear to direct my attention to his voice. "You take care up there, you hear?" I nod in reply and fight to show a grin despite my stomach's butterflies. Rising to his feet Frank is the last one to pass through the ship's threshold. "By the way." I turn my head to look to where he's standing in the shuttle's doorway. His face stares back with an *I didn't do it* grin. "Figured I'd better come clean, I altered your suit's measurements just enough to make it mildly uncomfortable. I didn't want you to forget about me while you are out there."

"You are a real prick, you know that?" I say with a smile accompanied with a wave of my left hand. On this note he closes and seals the cockpit's door. I turn back to the controls covering the panel positioned in front of my seat. Frank, the endless practical joker hasn't changed from when we were kids. Even after all of the destruction he still has his jokes. He's the one who kept me from taking a long walk off a short rooftop. If I'm being truly honest, he was the one who watched to make sure I didn't do anything stupid after that horrible night. The house went up so fast. There was nothing I could do and he held me back from blindly charging in. The house was filled with my whole family. I always knew I'd lose all I loved, but never figured on my parents, wife, and children going all at once. Frank literally is the sole person left on earth who's from my old life, my childhood friend. He's always been there to make sure I toe the line. Hope I can keep myself in check until we meet up on the other side. A jolting tug from the line of cable connecting the two crafts jerks my attention back to my current situation of my slumbering ship being dragged behind an aircraft for about a half hour before they detach the line.

2.

"We have reached our desired altitude. Awaiting orders to detach cable," reports the pilot's voice. I start flipping switches and pushing buttons until the console is light up with various information informing me the craft's engine is alive and purring.

"Icarus Twelve ready to detach," I reply into the microphone. My right hand is on the throttle waiting for the sudden drop before continuing my ascent.

"Detaching cable in three . . . two . . . one, release," counts the voice. With a momentary drop I push the throttle up on the craft's overpowering thrusters. With a minor push of the throttle the craft jumps a mile beyond the aircraft, which was previously ahead of me.

"Cool," I blurt out without realizing. Instinctively the moment I pushed up on the throttle I immediately pull back halfway in order to match my rate speed with that of the chauffeuring aircraft. The plane pulls alongside to my left. The voice again speaks into my earpiece.

"Good luck sir and godspeed," farewells the voice.

"Thanks. I sure could use some," I farewell back before pushing the throttle and lifting out of Earth's atmosphere and soon after its circling orbit. A few minutes later I've warped beyond Earth's neighboring stars even the once great Pluto. The warp drive will quicken my trip; however, the trip to Novae will still take six months to reach.

Space is a vast emptiness, all too easy to lose oneself, to forget your flight's purpose. Luckily I've got a chemical cocktail to put me to sleep until I've reached my destination. Liquid Cryo, it's a chemical mixture created by the same eggheads behind this mission. It's made to induce cryosleep without the hulking metal coffin.

The chemical injects straight into my arm's vein. I can't help, but to feel dizzy from the chemical's first introduction. While I hibernate my body slows to an almost catatonic state. Through it all my mind is kept active and alert. For six months my mind will function normally. Six months is a long time to be in suspended animation.

Quite awhile has passed and I've lost my bearings on time. Time means very little in my current state of being. I've spent most of it keeping myself sane with visions from past memories, my restructured memories of joy along with those of many remembered and forgotten sorrows.

I should have been with them. If I had, maybe I could have saved them. I said I had to work, but I went to the bar with Frank that night. I still remember the sound of my kids' screams as their voices were muffled by the searing flames engulfing the family homestead. I'm alone, because of my own selfish pursuits. My self-pity is broken by a computerized voice speaking into my ear. The chemical bleeds from out of my veins. The cockpit's metal blast shield retracts to be replaced by a vision of the blue plant named Novae.

"We've reached our destination point. Cryo system powering down," reports the computerized voice over and over. Even though my motor functions are not fully coherent I do manage to switch off the repetitive warning.

Reaching the planet's orbit I set myself into position to circle from above scanning for any signs of civilization. Unable to see any mass groupings I begin my descent into the planet's lower atmosphere. What I find odd is the planet is in full illumination yet there is no sun or great source of energy to emit such light. As I break through the outer shell of the planet's atmosphere I'm bombarded with an immensely overpowering white light. I cannot see anything in front of me. The light grows strongest just before I break through to see the blurring blues of the unpolluted oceans accompanied by the greenest of untouched forests.

I continue my descent to the standard height for aircraft back on Earth. It is here where I believe I have set my thoughts as to the source of the light. The upper atmosphere, which previously blinded me just moments ago, has something within creating a great glow. A glow so great it is able to illuminate the whole planet. I continue to proceed within the parameters of my mission to take readings of the world. Everything checks out, air – breathable, CO2 – acceptable. The planet is made of the exact same elements as Earth. I take a quick pass around the planet still looking for any evolved civilization and still I cannot find any cities or villages. I can't believe this planet is so perfect for human life. The two planets are identical. How's this even possible?

Sending a complete report of all the data collected back to Earth I precede to land in the middle of a vast and lush green field. Dropping the vessel's bottom hydraulic-operated bay door located at the center of the craft's undercarriage I take my first step onto Novae. The field is made of the most beautifully perfect knee-high grass I've ever seen ranking second only to the fields of my childhood homestead. The field is bordered on all sides by a bounty of healthy trees from oak to birch. I watch as a herd of white-tailed deer run across the field half a mile away. The herd is comprised of a dozen does, half a dozen fawns, and one massive twelve point buck leading the charge. I can only describe this place in one word *Paradise*. I continue my journey to touchdown on the planet's surface in search of finding and locating any signs of higher intelligence. From back inside I drive down the bay door, which at this time doubles for a ramp to aid in unloading the lithium battery-powered four-wheeler. I begin navigating across the untamed field towards the tree line. I reach the trees and proceed with caution. Uncertain as to what I will find within the shadow of the trees' canopy.

3.

After an hour or so of mapping my way along the terrain, I stop, turning off the quad's motor its low hum vanishes. The sound of a woodpecker distracts my thoughts. Turning to look I find the bird's red plumage is found with a simple ease set amongst the neighboring forest's brown and green landscape The woodpecker stops drilling into the tree before the bird flies over to land on my handle bars. The bird stares up at me tilting its head and sidesteps to its right. The woodpecker looks an awful lot like Woody.

I remember he was just an egg when I found him. I saw his mother get taken as she was returning with straw for his yet unfinished nest. A few weeks earlier the same hawk had taken his father. I rescued Woody and brought him home where I hatched and raised him. He would sit on my right index finger and rub his red feathers on the tip of my finger. Fate took him just as it had his parents. He was flying to my window when the speckle winged devil hawk swooped down and ended our friendship. I avenged them all by taking my pellet rifle and shooting the hawk dead. It fell from its nest with a crack and a bang to the ground.

"I wonder?" I remark before I hold out my right hand to the woodpecker. It tilts its small head to the left in a curious gesture. In one smooth movement the woodpecker hops onto my finger. The bird walks a moment as though dancing a jig. The bird rubs its feathered head on the tip of my index finger. "Woody!" The woodpecker looks into my eyes for a brief moment and with a flap of its red and black wings the bird returns to the previous tree. The woodpecker begins picking away at the tree for the tasty food harbored within. Woody is on this planet, but how is that even possible? I must still be suffering from space dementia or something. I must be hallucinating.

Returning to my previous distraction I drive until I come across a fence of thick brush looking to stretch for miles to my left and right. I guess I'm going through. I sure hope there are no hidden rocks buried in there. I pull back on the throttle. In seconds I'm being whipped by leaves and twigs. Ok, maybe not my brightest of ideas, but too late to stop now. The brush covers somewhere between fifty to a hundred feet before clearing into a ten-acre field. This field seems oddly familiar almost like I have been here before. I even remember the exact shape of the rock near the center of the field. It's strange, but the familiar feeling is too overwhelming for me to ignore. My thoughts again are distracted on hearing a faint creak followed by a wooded hinged bang. The sound reminds me of an old wooden screen door pulled back by its oversized spring only to slam shut against the door's steadfast frame. Turning to the sound I look across the field at its source. There it is what I traveled all this way in search of. On the far edge of the field stands a lone white three-story farmhouse. A mix of excitement and nervousness creeps across the whole of my body. I pull the throttle back to speed with a newfound insanity across the field in pursuit of the house.

The sturdy looking farmhouse is accompanied by a wraparound porch. The building's wood shingles are painted a flat white. Just like the farmhouse I grew up in as a child. I step off the four-wheeler and cautiously walk toward the porch's wooden staircase. While moving closer to the house I start to have the same feeling I had earlier. The only way I can describe it is to call it déjà vu for lack of a better word. I'm now twenty feet from the porch steps. I once more hear the creak and bang of a screen door from around the far side of the porch. It's followed by rhythmic tapping and creaking of farm boots stepping across an aged-stricken porch. The noise grows closer with each step from the far corner of the porch resting just in my line of sight. Its source is readying to reveal itself. I am ready for anything, anything that is, except for what I see next. A man appears from around the corner. He has short cropped hair and a great beard stretching almost halfway down his chest. He's followed by another person who's a fairly good-looking woman probably in her mid-thirties. Her long flowing red hair shines brightly in the light of the sky's glow. They stand above the porch's top step looking down on me. My brain races, because I swear I've seen them before.

"Welcome lad," says the farmer. He ends the greeting with a half grin. Only one person has ever called me lad. It is on this greeting I recall where I've seen these two before, in an old black and white photograph taken about five years after their marriage.

"Mom – Dad?" I reply in shock. No sooner are those words spoken I hear added voices belonging to two children followed closely by the loud smack of the screen door. The two children race around the corner and are stopped by my parents. They hold them back, due to the confusion filling my face from these new developments. The kids, they are mine, how? I heard their screams as the flames ravaged the house four years ago. Their cries have been burned into my mind ever since. "Jeremiah! Kiya! I've missed you so much." My words catch from the frog occupying my throat. Dropping to my knees with arms held wide I wait to hold them tight. My parents let go and the two children race down the steps nearly knocking me over as they fall into my open arms. I squeeze harder than I ever had before. Knowing deep down this must be a hallucination, but my mind does not care. Tears pour down my face as I hold them close.

"Come on dad. Let's go to my room and play a video game," suggests Jeremiah. He pulls on my hand begging me to go with him.

"Maybe later. We need to talk to your father a while longer," replies a voice I would know anywhere. It is the voice of my wife Christen. Looking up from my children's shoulders I see her standing at the corner looking at me watery-eyed. She continues to move to the top step making her way down until she stops at the bottom.

"Jeremiah. Why don't you and Kiya go to the kitchen table? I have fruit for you guys," she suggests without taking her eyes away from me.

"Fruit!" the two of them yell. Quickly they race up the stairs and vanish out of sight.

"What is this? Am I hallucinating?" I ask her, while she steps up to me.

"Well, if you are do you think we'd actually tell you?" she poses back after a moment's hesitation. "Why? Do you want to wake up?"

"No, I don't want to go, but why are you all here?" I ask.

"This is Heaven," replies my father.

"Heaven . . . how can that be? I'm on a planet called Novae millions of light years away," I counter.

"The last memory I remember is sitting in a fetal position in a burning house with no way out. My arms filled with Jeremiah and Kiya as the flames closed in. The next is a white light and here we were. We've spent all this time waiting for you," says Christen followed by a caressing hug. On the hug's release I look into her mesmer-izing eyes.

"But, I'm not dead. I am on a mission from Earth to explore this planet to see if it's suitable to support life. I need to get back to my ship and send a message," I explain. I spin around to face the four-wheeler.

"That won't be necessary, lad," says my father in a deep solemn voice.

"What are you talking about? I have a duty to Earth's last sur-vivors," I argue. I continue toward my vehicle. Climbing onto the four-wheeler I reach for the ignition key, but the key is not there. I know I left it in the ignition. From ahead of me I hear the sound of jingling keys. Looking up I see Frank standing beside the bottom step holding the keys in his right hand. Jumping off the four-wheeler I storm over to him.

"What the hell are you doing here?" I yell. I rip the keys from out of his hand and wait for an answer.

"That's what I was trying to tell you, lad" adds my father. Frank looks at me with the most serious look he's ever given.

"The Earth is gone George. It's too late. The planet self-destructed three months into your flight. The last we heard from you, you had gone into cryosleep," says Frank accompanied by resting his hand on my left shoulder.

"But how? I know the planet was in bad way, but they said we still had time?" I respond while feeling the planet's death weigh heavily upon the top of my shoulders. A great sadness fills me when I recall the other ships still out in space.

"I have to contact the other ships and tell them what has hap-pened," I say. Frank shakes his head.

"The other Icarus pilots are all gone too," replies Frank. "Icarus Ten hit an unknown asteroid belt before the pilot even went into stasis. Icarus Eleven lost cabin pressure and exploded in Earth's atmosphere. Icarus Thirteen landed on its destination, but the pilot came across hostile occupants. Let's just says we KNOW she didn't make it."

"Are you feeling alright? You've turned white as a ghost?" asks Christen. She puts her arm around me to help stable my shaky legs.

"I'm fine," I answer. After righting myself I look into her beautiful eyes. In honesty, my answer is farthest from the truth. A gut-wrenching realization falls upon me over what they are trying to say. You know that feeling you would get as a kid when you knew you'd done something you shouldn't have. You then hear the approaching footsteps of your all-knowing parents. At that very moment you knew you were in real trouble. Your body would cement in place unable to move a finger. No force of will could move you no matter how much you'd want to. The fear would keep its hold. Take that feeling and multiply it by two million more. From there you will know how I truly feel at this moment. I step away from my embracing helpers having to take a handful of minutes for myself. "What you are saying is the Earth is gone and the other three pilots are too?" My nervous state of being makes my voice tremble. I look up to all of them for conformation. Frank stands motionless, except to nod solemnly. "You mean I'm the last human alive in the universe?" Same as before I scan for conformation to my inquiry. They all stand motionless. A sudden sickness fills my soul making me dizzy and nauseated. "Am I dead?"

Dead Man's Dream

Listen to the words of the dead man's dream.
　　Pass the sentence that is deemed.
For all his crimes,
committed by this time.
No man will do the deed,
to the man in need.
They let him grow insane,
by the guilt building in his brain.
He awakes for a time,
then goes back into his mind.
Insane thoughts fill his head,
dreams of what once was, now is dead.
Locked inside his own guilt,
hiding from what should be felt.
This is the scene,
of the dead man's dream.

"I Really Love Your Eyes"

A brisk breeze blows through a patchwork of tricolor trees decorating Maine's mid fall landscape. These trees wrap around the off-ramp rest stop stationed between Lewiston and Augusta. These same trees shield the stop from the normally busy highway passing to its left. A lime green Volkswagen Beetle sits parked under the street lamp positioned out front of the old red brick building. The late night sky hangs shrouded in a blanket of thick clouds blocking the full moon's rays from shining through. The only visible illumination apart from the street lamp is the rest stop's fluorescent lights escaping from the interior through the building's windows and open doorways. The structure appears void of movement until a silhouette escapes from out of the doorway of light belonging to the men's room on the right. The silhouette is attached to a fairly attractive black haired young woman with broad shoulders towering near to six feet. She holds onto a handful of paper towels in her hands as she wipes off clear and crimson colored liquid. Once she's finished wiping her hands she pulls a black labelless lighter from out her right jacket pocket along with a small bottle of lighter fluid. Pouring an adequate amount on the ball of paper she drops it to the sidewalk's blacktop below her sneakers with a wet splat. In a sparked flicker of her lighter she leans over igniting the paper towels in a blaze of orange. The paper is half engulfed as she walks off the rest stop's sidewalk and into the parking lot.

She walks across the almost empty parking lot with keys in hand heading to the Volkswagen's trunk. With a metallic click the hood of the trunk unlocks. Placing her hand back into the same pocket where she acquired the lighter she removes a crimson-spotted brown paper bag. In the trunk's dark interior is a white cheap foam ice cooler. Opening the lid she places the spotted brown bag inside. Immediately after closing the trunk she moves around to the Volkswagen's driver side door. Opening the door she gently falls onto the seat and starts the near silent engine.

The Volkswagen exits the rest stop heading northbound on I-95 and increases in acceleration until she sets upon her desired speed of eighty-five miles an hour. *I love driving down the interstate at this time at night, because there are no slow pokes to get in my way.* Feeling a bit warm she rolls down the driver's window allowing her long black semi-curled hair to blow wildly in the mildly bitter night breeze flowing passed the side of her car. She drives this way for a little over an hour and a half before seeing the sign of her approaching exit ramp onto the Hogan Road in Bangor.

Upon exiting onto the off-ramp her eyes fall upon the twenty-four hour fifties-style dinner located across the street from the off-ramp. A growl in her stomach reminds her it hasn't been fed since noon and that was only half a bag of cream and onion chips.

"Fine" she tells herself, while turning to the right. She pulls into the dinner's nearly empty parking lot to park three spaces to the right of the entrance. Entering through the chrome polished door she stops with her back to it. Looking over the interior of the dinner she sees most of the patrons are too busy stuffing their faces to notice her. The room is filled by two rows of four circular tables spread across the main floor. Between the kitchen and the main room is a bar. The bar stretches the full length from wall to wall, accompanied with emplaced red leather swiveling stools. The other three walls of the dinner are covered by booths that can fit up to six adults comfortably in each. The seven patrons are in three different groups. The first is a bearded trucker weighing near to three hundred pounds wearing the stereotypical trucker ensemble including the multi-stained white t-shirt. He's rooted dead center of the bar working probably on his fifth cup of coffee. He's not sipping the cup of mud for its great taste. He's trying with great effort to talk himself into the skin-tight pants of the waitress in her late forties standing behind the counter. Next is an elderly couple who she reasons are the owners of the mid-sized RV parked outside. Looking at the couple's clothes she can guess they have only recently retired and are attempting to have one final hurrah with the remainder of their short-lived freedom. The third is a family comprised of two parents and two extremely well-behaved little girls. Her power of deduction suggests the Florida plated SUV with the strapped bags secured to the cab's roof belongs to this happy bundle. They dress like non-local tourists with their perfectly natural tans from multiple days under sun-baked skies. Its mid-October in Maine and the last of the sun-bathing days has long since gone until their return next summer. Next summer feels like a lifetime away with the unknown number of Nor'easter storms that will come to blanket this state white with wet heavy packs of snow.

After having completed her survey of the patrons she makes her way over to the large red-leather booth in the far right corner. While waiting for the waitress to arrive she looks over a cardboard cut-out advertising three customizable milkshakes. Within five minutes the forty year old waitress is standing center to her table holding out the dinner's menu with her left hand. Taking the menu from the waitress she opens to the middle looking over the 'Day's Specials'.

"Would you like me to get your drink while you decide?" asks the waitress looking down on the newly-arrived patron.

"Yes, how about -- do you have Pepsi or Coke?" she asks.

"Pepsi," she returns without the slightest pause.

"Alright Mountain Dew then, please?" she answers. The waitress scribbles the drink type on her order pad and returns the pad into her apron tied around her waist.

"Ok. I'll be right back," the waitress says before turning to go back to the opening to the side of the bar. Once behind the bar she grabs up a yellow-tinted glass with her right hand. The heavy set trucker tries to rekindle their earlier conversation. Ultimately, he leaves empty-handed when she tells his slovenly person that she was only warming him up to get a better tip of gratuity. The female traveler can't help, but snicker at witnessing this scene of disappointment and humiliation on the trucker's face. She turns back to reading the night's specials, but in the end decides to choose the bacon and Swiss cheeseburger. While waiting on the waitress to return she sets the cardboard flier on top of her refolded menu and again looks over the three house milkshakes for only $4.95, plus tax.

"That better be a really good milkshake for four bucks," she thinks out loud. Out of the corner of her eye she sees a pair of legs heading to her booth. She looks up to see a young man bringing her soda and sets the glass on the table slightly to her right. He's not gorgeous by any stretch of the imagination, but he's better looking against the norm. However, there's something that keeps her from being able to take her eyes away from him. She can sense his nervousness grow due to her intensely fixed stare. He gives her a nervous grin with wandering eyes caused from his uneasiness. This observation helps her to realize what it is that's attracting her. It's the color of his eyes. They are the most attractive and mesmerizing shade of green she's ever seen.

"Are you ready to order?" he asks. On this development she breaks her stare to open the menu to her chose.

"Yes. I would like the bacon and Swiss cheeseburger. I would like to add lettuce and tomatoes to it," she answers as though the awkward connection had never taken place. She holds out the dinner menu hesitating long enough to take one last look into those gorgeous one-of-a-kind eyes.

"I really love your eyes," she says in a passionate and longing tone. The young man takes a slight step back from the booth and frowns in the center of his brow in an expression of uncomfortable nervousness.

"Thank you I guess?" he says in an elongated voice.

"I mean, I've never seen anyone's eyes look as beautiful as yours. I would really love for my boyfriend to have them. Can I have your eyes?" she adds in a heightened pitch of excitement. It's the kind of tone children make on Christmas morning in anticipation of waking their snoozing parents so they can open their presents.

"Oh yeah -- sure," he says in a sarcastic tone. With that uncomfortable closer to the conversation the young man simply nods his head, forces a grin, and moves as quickly as he can from the unsettling conversation originated by the psychotic patron. Moving out of earshot he mumbles under his breath. "Crazy freak -- man don't I hate the graveyard shift." She sits in wait for his return. Hoping to get another chance to look into those eyes she lusts for with an uncontrollable desire. They are the kind of eyes she would definitely need to build her ideal mate. After fifteen excruciating minutes of waiting her food arrives to her booth, but it's brought by the previous waitress.

"Where's the man who took my order?" she asks.

"Chris? Oh, he was just covering for me for a few so I could finish my last cig. Just between us he's not even supposed to step out from behind the kitchen," the waitress answers as she sets the white plate on the center of the placemat. "If you are interested? Let me save you some heartache, girl. He's engaged to a very nice pretty young thing and nothing could ever tear those two apart. Do you understand what I'm saying, hon." She nods in recognition to humor the meddlesome clucking hen. "Well, at any rate. Enjoy the meal -- he made it." She turns back to the bar to continue her other nightly duties.

The waitress walks passed the bar and enters through the doorway leading to the dinner's kitchen. She stops to the right of Chris, who's leaning over the large stainless steel dual sink half full of dishes. He continues cleaning the dishes in an attempt to empty the sink so he can drain it for the last time of the night.

"You were right. She's all about you, son. I told her what you asked me too, but I don't think she'll listen," she explains. "Be careful. This time of night we only get two kinds of people, drifters and the crazies. I can tell you from my years of experience in the trade. From the vibe she's putting out. She's no drifter." Following her advice she leaves the kitchen to wait on the remaining patrons.

She works on her cheeseburger at a slug's pace thinking all the while about those gorgeous green eyes she has to have. All throughout eating her burger she keeps a keen eye peeled for any remote signs of Chris passing by the kitchen's open doorway. Suddenly a thought pops into her mind like someone backhanded her upside the head. The thought reminds her about the perishable contents held within the brown paper bag in the cooler located in her Volkswagen's trunk. Right then and there her hand raises for the check and in a blink consumes the last bites of her burger. The waitress places the bill face down on the booth's table. Digging into the front pocket of her denim jeans she removes three twenty dollar bills folded in half. Setting one of the twenties from the bundle on top of the unturned bill she grabs her yellow-tinted glass to take one final mouthful of soda before bursting out the dinner's front door heading back to her lime green car.

Later that night in the early morning hours of six-thirty, the graveyard shift comes to a close allowing the shifts forced labor to escape until next time. Chris drags his feet out the front door heading back to his apartment for a few hours sleep. He stops to stand beside the driver side door to his 1967 Mustang fixer-upper and falls onto the seat. The mustang starts with a loud grinding churn. The sound transforms into a low-end grumble due mainly to the large hole in the car's muffler pipe. Pulling out of the parking lot he turns to the left gradually pick up speed in the direction of his warm bed and even warmer fiancée. With his thoughts on what lies ahead he doesn't notice the lime green Volkswagen positioned across the parking lot. Behind the wheel sits a tall and dark silhouette. After he advances a fair, though small, distance from his hourly prison the Volkswagen pulls out to follow. The pair head along his routine route for twenty minutes until the '67 Mustang steers down a dead-end road off of downtown Main Street. The Mustang pulls off and onto an oversized driveway belonging to a two-story duplex apartment building. The lime green Volkswagen stops on the side of the dead-end drive two houses down from his apartment.

Her eyes follow Chris exiting from his Mustang to advance up the exterior gray-painted staircase leading to his second floor apartment. Reaching the top of the stairs he's greeted by a small and curvy red-haired young woman in a thin silky robe. It takes no reasonable difficulty to deduce this is all she is wearing. She plants her lips on his upon his arrival at the door. They enter the apartment with their lips still locked tightly accompanied by the door closing silently behind them. Calmly she waits for his fiancée to leave for her day's errands.

At seven-fifteen the man living in the first floor apartment leaves for work. She concludes this guess by the simple fact he's wearing a company uniform. Quarter after eight is when her wait finally pays off, because the fiancée exits the apartment and descends the exterior steps. She walks with caution due to her high-heels, which accompany her dressy bank teller type ensemble. After stepping off the bottom step she opens the door of a blue Neon parked to the left of Chris's Mustang. Pulling out onto the dead-end road she drives mere inches from her fiancée's stalker with only two panels of glass separating their interaction. The fiancée gives her a questioning glance of passing curiosity. She continues down the road picking up speed all the while moving further away from their apartment. Only after the blue Neon turns left onto the intersecting street does the driver's door of the Volkswagen open and its inhabitant steps out. Casually she strolls up to and across the duplex's driveway before climbing the stairs with silent ease until reaching the upper deck. With the turn of the door-knob she finds the door to be unlocked. On this discovery she enters without any effort needed through the apartment's threshold in three firm steps. Closing the door she freezes stiff to listen with heightened hearing to locate where in the apartment he's currently residing. From a closed door at the end of a short hall she hears the sound of swirling water flowing down a porcelain waterslide. She crouches behind a red and green striped flannel-patterned couch positioned directly in front of a 42 inch LED flat screen.

Chris exits the bathroom to enter into the living room. He stops to the front right side of the couch. The intruder is concealed behind the large piece of furniture she pulls from out of her green military jacket pocket a white cloth followed by a clear medical bottle with blue and red lettering on its label. Covering the now open bottle with the white cloth she tips the container just enough to allow it to become wet. After screwing the cap on the bottle she waits for him to sit on the couch or to give her the opportunity to make her move. In three steps he breaches the distance from the couch to the television to set his wallet and keys into a porcelain skull set to the front right of the screen. From here he turns to move into the adjacent room where his queen-sized bed is situated. His back swings to the couch giving her the chance she's been hoping for. Jumping with all the grace of a cheetah over the chunk of wood and cushions she lands gracefully behind Chris's bare heels. A few steps later she is on his back forcing the white cloth over his mouth and nose with her other arm locking around his neck. In desperation he tries to shake her off. However, she is too well-trained to this progression of events and in turn is amply suitable for this strenuous task. Finally the chemical having taken effect causes him to fall unconscious to the ground with a hard smack.

"Time to remove the dead weight and claim what was promised," she mumbles. She folds the white cloth and returns it to her jacket pocket along with the waiting bottle. She grins as she begins to pull him toward the room containing the sheet-covered mattress. "I love this new stuff. It works soooo much better than the good ol' pipe to the back of the head. It preserves them better too."

She lays out all the tools needed on the bedside table. She removes from her other jacket's pocket a one-inch pill-shaped capsule. Snapping the capsule in half she swipes it twice under Chris's nostrils. He awakes with a jolt and looks around with a dazed expression. He discovers he's strapped to the bedposts by various kinds of fabric knotted tightly around each of his limbs. Turning his head to the right he makes wide-eyed contact with the person who assaulted him.

"You . . . what do you want from me? Why am I tied up? Let me go," he says in a steadily growing voice, while wiggling back and forth in a vain attempt to try to pull any of his limbs free. To stop his line of questions and demands she inserts a ball of cloth to gag his endless talking.

"I don't want anything you can't part with. I'm not going to kill you," she states in a calm voice. "If your heart were to give out it isn't really my fault, understand? Like I said to you earlier, I love your eyes and I want my boyfriend to have them. Besides you said I could have them. No taking backzees." She stops her speech to stare lovingly into his pools of green. "Oh yes. So you don't hurt yourself. I'm going to give you a drug to immobilize you for a little while. Don't worry you will be awake and aware. I feel like this is a particularly special thing we should both share. The others who've been in your place, I like to think they found themselves after it was all said and done. I won't lie; some of them have died for one reason or another. None of it was ever my fault! I don't think its fair the news calls me a freak or sicko, and I'm definitely not a murderer. They died, because their bodies weren't strong enough. I never took any major organs. I know. I went to school to become a nurse. I never made it passed the first semester, because of my anxiety issues. But, I at least tried! That should count for something, right?" While ranting blindly she's injecting the immobilizing chemical into one of his pulsing veins. A couple of minutes pass before his fighting and murmuring halts to a stop. "Let's get started. We've only a short time until soon-to-be wifey comes home. We don't want her coming to the wrong conclusions as to why I'm on your bed with you," She follows this comment with a giddy laugh and wry smile. Grabbing a tool from off the bedside table she holds it over one of his wide eyes. "Let's begin by popping the eyes out of their sockets." She speaks as if she's talking herself through the steps. The last thing he feels before blacking out is a metallic instrument pushing in above his left eye joined immediately by unimaginable pain. His skull fills with the muted sound of gut-wrenching screams.

The sun is in full life with the orange ball of flame mingling with the sporadic puffs of white clouds of vapor over a sea of blue sky. The duplex sits in quiet peace, which hides the horrifying scene lying within. Suddenly, as if, to break the current atmosphere the second floor apartment's door opens and the eye collecting woman exits with the door closing silently behind her. She crosses the driveway to reach her Volkswagen and again opens the trunk. She pulls from her jacket pocket a brown bulging paper bag and places it into the cooler located in the trunk's storage compartment. The ice inside has melted to clear liquid soaking the bag on contact. Closing the trunk she moves to the driver's door. At this very moment, the same blue Neon turns down the dead-end road on its return to their apartment. Once the woman in the blue Neon is out of her car and ascending her way up the staircase the lime green Volkswagen performs a U-turn. The driver casually steers to the intersecting street at the end of the road. She drives roughly ten minutes before she is passed by an ambulance accompanied by two police cruisers with sirens wailing zooming by in the direction of the dead-end street. She sits pulled over onto the shoulder and watches them disappear from her rearview mirror.

Later that night after she's been home long enough to take a shower and have a good meal. She shuffles into her living room to read for a short while before heading off to bed. The fireplace is blazing nicely filling the room with walls of dancing shadows. She sits on a dark brown recliner with a standing lamp towering over to the right of her head. It's enough illumination to allow her to read without disturbing the cozy atmosphere created by the dancing fire. She stops reading to watch the sway of the flames dance along the wall's smooth surface. She reminds herself to this being one of her main reasons for wanting this house. She loves a real fireplace, to her nothing else can compare. Turning back to her open book she once more works on reading her historical romance novel. A significant length of time passes in a shroud of silence when she laughs at something in the book.

"Honey, when I'm done with this book you should definitely read it," she speaks with her head tilting toward the fireplace. She looks to the mantel where four crudely constructed shelves are located. On the bottom shelf dead center is a pickle jar filled with some kind of clear, but cloudy liquid. Floating in the liquid is a pair of human lips. The next shelf up contains three of the same pickle jars filled with different body parts positioned from left to right; ear, nose, ear. The next shelf up holds a single jar containing a pair of newly-acquired green eyeballs accompanied by a fair amount of their stems. On the top shelf sits a freshly scalped chunk of short ginger blonde hair styled into a forest of spikes. "Oh honey, your hair is starting to lose its firmness. I'll pick up some more gel tomorrow. I know it's corny to say, but you are the most perfect boyfriend in the world." She returns her view back to her book with a great smile from ear to ear, as if, the body parts have spoken to her. "I love you too, sweetie."

Phantom Shield

"Doug, just the one I was looking for," greets Burt, a man in his early thirties. He is dressed in an off-the-rack gray business suit with fuzzy brown hair hanging off his perfectly shaped skull.

Looking for me, why?" returns Doug. His wardrobe is one of a custom-tailored blue suit. It's the only one of its kind he owns. He could never afford to have one made on his monthly income. The only reason he has this one is because it was a birthday present from a wealthy ex-girlfriend. While waiting for an answer he continues on his previous course passing his young energetic assistant manager to arrive at his cubicle.

"Mike was supposed to be going to the car expo in Chicago, but his younger sister was hit by a car. She's in critical condition," sputters out the young assistant manager at a heightened rate of speed. "So I need you to replace him at the expo."

"Sure. I'd like to help Burt, but I have three customers coming in today to finalize their purchases," he replies.

"I have no problem taking care of them for you, and don't worry I won't take your commission," says Burt. Doug can see there's no way out of this assignment.

"When is the flight?" asks Doug trailed directly by a sigh of surrender.

"Take off is at twelve-thirty. Five hours from now," answers Burt with a crooked grin. "It's a five day expo, so make sure to check out the new sports models."

"I guess . . . I'd better head home to pack," remarks Doug. He starts to advance three steps back to the front door when Burt calls again.

"You might need this," he comments with his right arm extended to show a small rectangular paper folder containing the round trip to Chicago. Having to once more backtrack to his snot-nosed supervisor he takes the ticket before moving to the front door on his return trip home to pack so he can arrive at the airport in time.

Following a fifteen minute trip across this small bustling city he pulls onto his paved driveway in front of his single car garage. Stepping through the side door to the house, which leads into the kitchen he startles his half-dressed wife. She's the envy of most men, if not, all of his friends. Though he's in his mid-forties, his wife is ten years his younger. She's put on a few pounds since they married ten years back. As the pounds would have it, they merely amplify her already satisfying curves.

"What are you doing back from work?" she asks with eyes wide. Leaning against the kitchen's middle island she holds a blue mug with steam rising up to vanish in the air above.

"Burt's sending me out to a car expo in Chicago I'll be gone for five days," he states in an emotionless tone. A wide smile spreads across her face on hearing this news.

"That's good isn't it?" she asks. "That's normally a task handed to the manager or at least the senior salesperson."

"I may not be the senior salesman, but I'm definitely the oldest one there," he remarks in a scoffed tone. She gives him a stern glare to his verbal downgrading.

"You're older than them. So what? Who cares?" she snaps. "I look at it this way, if Burt is sending you to the expo there must be a good reason. Why don't you thank that gift horse instead of trying to put a bullet in its head?"

"Fine, I have to go pack," he surrenders. The couple shares a passionate embrace. She breaks from his moist lips.

"Do you have the time?" she asks. Her eyes stare longingly into his beautiful blue eyes.

"The plane doesn't leave until twelve-thirty," he replies, her eyes glance at the kitchen's analog wall clock located in the center of a plastic mold forming a pudgy chef. The clocks black hands are positioned at quarter after nine. Turning her gaze back to Doug she gives him a grin and once again locks her wanting lips with his. With a gentle lift he sits her on the kitchen's island. Her legs wrap around his waist. With skilled hands she starts to help remove his jacket and shirt. The whole time their lips do not part, while they say goodbye the only way a passionate couple does when forced with five days of forthcoming separation.

With their prolonged goodbye finished and his bags packed he arrives at the airport with two hours to spare. He sits waiting to board the plane in the airport lobby for the next hour and a half. After boarding the aircraft they sit motionless on the tarmac for a further forty-five minutes. The plane rolls down the asphalt runway to an ever increasing speed until its bloated frame lifts into the air. The climb pushes upward until the plane has reached its desired altitude, miles above the hard unforgiving ground. Only now does his flight advance without any further complications. They touch down in Chicago followed by Doug quickly shuffling through customs to the airport's taxi alley. After occupying a cab he is taken to his hotel. The hotel is positioned only a couple blocks from the civic center where the expo is being held.

Upon entering the lobby, he finds the sitting area filled by various levels of car salespersons newly arrived like him for the expo. Doug signs the registry book placed ahead of him on the front counter with a keycard placed to the book's right belonging to his waiting accommodations. Taking a short shower to scrub off the remaining leftovers from the trip he feels rejuvenated and decides to walk the blocks between the hotel and civic center. At five-thirty the expo's spokesman greets the show's attending visitors. In his speech he outlines the five days of demonstrations and talks of the show's top events. Doug picks up a program folder of the expo with the show's detailed list of events along with a bundle of advertising freebies, mostly pens and magnets.

On the morning of the second day, Doug is dressed by five-thirty and walks half a block in the opposite direction of the civic center to order a coffee and a breakfast sandwich from a local establishment he was told about yesterday. The first two-thirds of the day go by without a hitch with him occupied by checking out the newest model Mustang, Dodge, along with a whole new line of Honda Hybrids. Most of these legendary car titles have been given new plastic shells covering the same mechanical inner workings. The specific vehicle, which caught his eye in the expo's info folder is a vehicle equipped with a new state-of-the-art collision prevention device. From first glance, the car looks as near to any other new model rolling off the assembly line. The salesman for the model notices Doug's intrigued interest and with his current sales pitch plummeting, he gives his best greeting. The salesman pounces on the new arrival in three extended steps without Doug receiving the slightest warning.

"Good afternoon, sir," he greets in a smile causing his face to vanish. Doug turns his attention to the salesman returning his own smile accompanied by a single nod. "Isn't this a modern marvel? With this new invention, car accidents will be a thing of the past, a bedtime story to tell one's grand kids."

"What makes it so state of the art?" questions Doug. "It doesn't look any different from half the models here."

"First. What's your name, sir?" asks the skillful fast-talking salesman working to bait his hook.

"Doug," he answers.

"Ok, Doug. Have you ever heard of ectoplasm?" asks the man.

"You mean the stuff left behind by ghosts, supposedly?" replies Doug with a puzzled expression.

"Exactly," he agrees with a clap of his thick hands. "My company's scientists have found a way to catch and harness this very ectoplasm left behind by ghosts. The device is for lack of a better term, fused with the 'plasm to help protect the vehicle and its occupants in the case of collision. Sensors are located three-sixty around the vehicle, which senses when a collision is imminent. The vehicle and all within are ghosted until the oncoming collision has safely passed. With the threat having passed, the device deactivates with no harm to person or machine."

"How did they manage to harness the ectoplasm?" probes Doug.

"That, I do not know. I'm only the salesman," he replies. "But you must see what a deal this is? At one hundred and fifty thousand dollars you're not buying a car, but the peace of mind and comfort of knowing you are protecting the ones you cherish from any unnecessary harm." The salesman nods, his sight lands on the wedding band on Doug's left hand.

"For one hundred and fifty thousand dollars, I could buy a caravan of vehicles," counters Doug.

"You are right about that," the salesman agrees. "But, none of them are equipped with Phantom Shield. What do you think? Are you ready to fill out the paperwork?" Doug has to give credit to the man. He's a natural-born salesman and knows how to maneuver a mark, as if, he has a psychic sense. The two men continue this line of banter for an additional twenty minutes before Doug finalizes his signature on the empty lines at the bottom of the contract. The two men part ways with the final exchange being one of Doug's personal checks made out for fifty thousand dollars and zero cents.

The next two days at the expo go by without any real interest to note. On the last half of the fourth day Doug decides to catch an early flight home and spend the last paid day of the expo at home with his waiting wife. He's barely able to board the six-thirty flight before its departure is granted. Unfortunately, unlike before this flight is not a straight shot home. He has to catch a connecting flight out of some no-name backwater town. Its airport is just big enough to accommodate larger aircraft. Instead of touching down at his hometown at eight, due to the connecting flight's delay, he reaches his destination quarter past twelve.

Pulling into his driveway he finds a silver sports car parked beside his wife's dark green SUV. A mixed expression of disbelief and realization cascades down his face. He recognizes the invading vehicle as it belongs to Burt. Doug's thoughts don't need two or three guesses as to why it's here at this late hour. After opening the door of his car Doug steps out and advances into the house on noiseless steps.

The next several hours in the kitchen he drinks liquid spirit to help him gain the courage for the forthcoming confrontation. Soon after six forty-five the recently intermingled couple descends the stairs in only their basic attire. Making the corner to enter through the kitchen's archway his wife enters first. Burt's arms are wrapped around her waist with his lips traveling all along her neck.

"Good morning, honey," greets Doug to break through any stilled silence that would have befallen the room once they had notice him. She jumps in response to seeing her husband of ten years sitting on a stool beside the middle island with a three-quarters empty bottle of whiskey in his left hand. "Burt – I'd ask if you'd like some breakfast, but I can see you've already eaten."

"Doug –" she says in a stammer.

"Please," interrupts Doug with his unoccupied hand raised to show its open palm facing them. "Save it. On this epiphany-inducing night I've realized this isn't the first time, is it?" Her mouth opens to speak than closes once nothing comes out.

"Why are you not in Chicago?" demands Burt in his best supervisorial tone.

"I'm sorry you're not my manager here, Burt. So, I'd appreciate if you'd be seen and not heard," he snaps with an aggressive tone. Burt's face turns white from the shock of the direct order. Doug holds his view on Burt for a couple more beats before shifting back to the woman still wrapped in his arms. "The last day of the expo was a bullshit day. Nothing of any real interest was being displayed and I decided to start for home early." He rises from off the stool and sets the unfinished bottle on the island's counter. "I'll be going, I guess. Once I've figured out my living arrangements I'll return for my things."

Doug swivels his feet on their heels to center back on the door he stepped through hours earlier. On reaching the door and rotating the handle with his right hand he spins his head to set his view once more on his one-time wife. "Honey, you were right about one thing. This expo was a good opportunity for someone."

By early afternoon he returns to the now empty house to gather the basics he'll take back to his modest hotel room with a high weekly rate. In the driveway on his arrival he sees the newly purchased silvery gray car equipped with Phantom Shield technology. In the glove compartment he finds the needed paperwork to legalize the vehicle. Following a quick trip to city hall he loads his new wheels with his meager belongings. Doug sits on the seat located behind the steering wheel. At first he looks the interior over to see everything is a flat black. All the display instruments are positioned in the middle of the dashboard. Directly behind the wheel is a moderate-sized square open shelf. After inserting the key he turns the ignition and in response the engine emits a quiet hum. He notices on the bottom right of the speedometer an extra indicator light. It's light blue with an image of a generic ghost holding a medieval shield. Doug can't help, but grin at the comical symbol attached to such a serious state-of-the-art protection system.

Backing out of the driveway he rolls along this quiet urbanite environment. The car handles just as smoothly as any new vehicle should. He drives with leisure for five blocks before his cellphone rings from a source he's been dreading. Extending his right hand from the steering wheel he presses the green TALK button and waits to hear her voice come out through the car's speakers.

"Yes? What do you want?" he asks with his eyes pointed straight ahead.

"Doug?" she replies with a slight crackle from the speakers.

"It's me. I don't know who else you were expecting to answer my cell?" he remarks with a sharp tongue.

"I called to explain and see how you're doing," she says with apparent hesitation. "I never meant for –"

"Save it Lorraine it's done. I don't need to hear your justification for cheating. I already know what's important," he interrupts.

"Are you ok?" she asks with a sympathetic voice.

"About as good as any other man who found his wife screwing his boss in his house can be," he replies. "What is it you're hoping this conversation will accomplish?" In the silence following his question he hears another faint voice leak from the speakers. Three words into the unknown voice Doug recalls who the nasally voice belongs to. "Where are you?"

"I'm at home," she answers in a tearful voice.

"You're at our house calling me to apologize for cheating on me and all the while the prick is standing right beside you?" he hollers with his eyes burning at the phone in a vain attempt to show her his anger.

"Doug, there's no reason to –" she says before he cuts her off once more.

"Shout? Oh, I think this is the perfect time to yell," he says at a higher volume. He guesses this time his yell must have hurt, because he hears her release a sound signaling a sharp pain. With his mind and attention distracted he does not notice he's pulled into the other lane. A blue king cab truck is only seconds ahead of Doug's bumper. His attention is redirected by a screaming truck horn, which is quickly growing louder. "Oh crap!"

Right before the two metal cases are to collide a strange feeling washes over him. It's as though time has actually slowed and everything he sees has turned a neutral gray. Looking down at the dashboard he finds the once elusive icon of the ghost holding a shield now glows bright. The icon is the only thing in his surrounding sight, which is a different color than gray.

The ghosting starts at the front of the nearing collision. The transitional point of transparency moves in a straight line across the vehicle like a lit scanner bar of a copy machine. The line travels across the full length of the hood in a gradual advance toward the windshield. Doug's mouth hangs open in awe at the sight unfolding before him.

The sweeping transformation reaches the windshield and passes into the car's interior. He watches in frozen shock as everything within transforms into a ghostly shadow including his own physical body. Through the rearview mirror he watches the line of transparency leave out the back window. He notices his sight is left unaltered by the transformation, except of course for the dulled gray tint of color blanketing everything in his vision.

The front of the car emerges from out of the back bumper of the larger truck's tailgate and begins to rematerialize in the same manner as it had vanished. Once the car has fully materialized time appears to have returned to its normal speed. At the first vacant parking space to his right he pulls in ending in a sudden jolted stop due to the car's sensitive brakes. Sitting in silence with a wide-eyed expression he allows time to pass on, while his mind tries in desperation to sort through the information collected from this experience. Doug can't help to feel as though his soul is possessing someone else's body. It feels as though the experience has separated his spiritual self from his physical self. A haunting voice attracts the attention of Doug's shocked and heightened hearing. His eyes fall to the plastic and wire device held in its holder to the left of the car stereo. By the time his thoughts can decide to speak the only sound emitting from the stereo's speakers is the hollow sound of digital silence. Pressing the red END button stops the hollow sound from the speakers. With hands of needles he wipes them over his body to make physically sure everything is as it should be. Besides the feeling of separation the only other side effect he feels is of extreme nausea. On this unnerving experience he returns to his room to eat dinner, if he can, followed immediately by crawling into his rented mattress. This is an added difficulty, because it is as comfortable as a cloth-covered brick.

Six months have passed since his first experience with Phantom Shield. The divorce has taken its toll on Doug and especially his wallet. Three weeks after finding Burt and his wife playing paddy cake, he was let go with no true reason given. For Doug the only shock was that it took so long to happen. The greater shock occurred over the next following weeks. With the stellar resume he had he can't find a sales job or anything of equal stature who'd hire him. He had to return to one of his first jobs he had back when he was fresh out of high school with a childhood friend. Luckily, for him he kept the friendship going after he left the business. The pay at the tire and lube service station was a substantial decrease from the dealership, but still it was income he desperately needed. Both the divorce and his weeks of unemployment having crippled his years of accumulated savings.

After a particular busy day at the station he sits on the driver's seat of his car in route to his monthly paid abode to drown his sorrows away in a tall glass of spiked tea waiting in his fridge. No thanks to his soon-to-be ex-wife he has been able to keep on top of the car's remaining payments. He has had no real expenses except for his rent, lawyer, and a few bucks to sustain his decaying life. While advancing down a moderately filled section of Interstate 95 toward his exit ramp, he cranks his favorite and only radio station - 95.7 WTZV, the Wolf. The factory speakers are straining from the high level of the volume, but they are able to maintain. In the middle of a southern rock song it muffles down to be over-powered by a metallic series of beeps indicating a call is incoming. Without removing his sight from the straight stream of asphalt he extends his right hand from the wheel to press the green TALK button on his cellphone.

"Hello?" he greets to the unknown voice on the other end of the line.

"Doug?" returns a masculine voice with a Texas accent through the speakers. Doug can tell by the accent it's his attorney.

"Yes, Darren how's the settlement coming along? Is she ready to finalize?" he asks. Though his voice is high in spirits, his stomach is filled beyond capacity with fluttering butterflies.

"Almost," answers the voice with a hesitant break. This causes the swarm of butterflies to stir into a frantic frenzy. He turns down along his spiraling exit ramp to pull onto the traffic flowing highway of Route Nine. "She's agreed to all you've suggested, but she wants spousal support. Her lawyer says that it's a non-negotiable condition and if you don't agree they'll see us in court."

"She's living with Burt! I know it for a fact," argues Doug with a dumbfounded expression. "I'm giving her everything we have including half of the savings, or at least the last of my savings. Now she wants me to keep paying for her to whore around? No. I won't agree to that, it's not fair."

"I agree with your last statement, but this is how these things usually play out," remarks Darren's voice. "We can go to court, but I want your full attention, Doug. IF we go to court chances are they're going to look at the fact you've supported her through your ten years of marriage and they are more than likely going to award her the support."

"What percentage would you give to that verdict?" Doug asks as he attempts to take in a few calming breathes.

"I'd give it. Eighty-five percent in her favor," answers the lawyer. "Courts generally give sympathy to domesticated housewives who are thrust out into the big wide world. Look. Don't rush to a decision now. Think it over and get a hold of me. Talk to you later." The speakers click to trail off into a digital hollow silence. With a heavy hand Doug presses the red END button to silence the silence. Large tears hang from the tip of his lower lashes before cascading down his fleshy cheeks.

At the other end of the four mile straightaway he sees a fast-approaching semi-truck hauling cut tree trunks. Doug's hands, which are positioned at ten and two of the steering wheel, tighten their noose until his knuckles turn white. The truck breaches the mile marker from Doug's vehicle. With a slight turn of the wheel his car crosses the single broken yellow line to stare into the semi's chrome grill. The driver of the truck lays full force on his horn, but instead of deterring Doug. Doug forces the pedal of the accelerator fully to the floor.

It's not until his surroundings bleed out into the neutral gray is he reminded as to what vehicle he's driving. At this point of understanding a deeper despair causes him to realize he can't affectively commit suicide this way. The transparency sweeps across the vehicle as it had months before. The car begins to pass behind the truck's grill, which shows only a reflection in its chrome of the car's backside. The vehicle passes at what feels to be a much slower pace, however, the semi's size is vastly larger in length compared to the king cab truck of the last incident. The front of Doug's car exits from the trailer's rust-coated metal bumper. The car's rematerialization is able to reach the windshield before the front bumper once again starts to ghost due to a red SUV located half a car length behind the semi-truck. Doug watches helplessly as a third of his car is materialized with the other two-thirds remaining translucent. It is at this moment he sees the coming horror lying before him. Behind the truck there are nine differing vehicles all in close proximity to one another. In vain, he turns the wheel to steer himself back into his proper lane. The attempt is useless with the Phantom Shield activated. The device has taken control of the vehicle's instruments for safety reasons.

For the witnesses watching this scene unfold, the whole event passes to its conclusion in under a minute. The transparent car fully materializes on passing through the ninth and final vehicle's rear bumper. Doug's car slows to a stop along the ditch to the road's left side. The cars' passengers who've witnessed the ghosting car stop and gawk in wide-mouthed silence. The bear of a man who drives the semi-truck walks back to the mysterious car to find the driver's door ajar. Reaching the door he opens the hinged metal to its widest point to allow his own wide physique to peer inside unobstructed. The vehicle sits vacant with nobody within, alive or dead. The trucker looks back over the stretch of road, but can't see any sign of the car's previous occupant. With the arrival of the sheriff and two of his deputies they proceed to take eyewitness statements and contact information from each.

One by one, the witnesses leave the terrifying scene. Among the departing vehicles is a large double cab truck, which was the fifth vehicle behind the semi. Two men sit in the cab in route to the main storage facility to unload the truck bed of the machinery owned by their construction company before heading home for the day. They talk about the unbelievable and unforgettable event they were a part of. Their conversation is cut off by the truck's radio abruptly turning on without any assistance. The digital dial switches through the channel frequencies until it stops on its chosen frequency. Both men stare at the possessed radio with equally spooked expressions.

"This is ninety-five point seven WTZV – the Wolf. We play all the classic rock you crave. Let's start our next five pack with a song that was a favorite of the American G.I.'s in Vietnam," says the station's DJ followed with a pair of thumbing guitars playing the song's haunting intro. One of the two men tries to turn off the radio with no luck. He presses the eject button to remove the stereo's face plate and successfully disconnects it from the radio.

"Weird -- it's never done that before," comments the driver. Silence fills the truck's interior until they arrive at the office ten minutes later.

A couple days following the incident, a representative from the car company arrives to obtain a copy of the police report and to retrieve the vehicle. He interviews three of the witnesses who saw the most. Completing his fact gathering he returns to the airport to catch the next flight back to Chicago. While waiting for his flight to begin boarding he contacts his supervisor to relay what he learned of the incident. After pressing the green receiver icon associated with the appropriate contact number he raises the phone to his ear.

"John here, I reviewed the incident report and questioned the top witnesses as indicated by the protocol procedures and I found it's the same basic issue," he says to the silent voice on the other end of the line. He listens silently at the voice coming back through the phone's receiver. "Yes. He tried to exit the vehicle. At least that's what I've determined, because when it materialized the driver's door was open wide." He again waits patiently listening to what his boss is saying on the other end. "I've been saying all along we need an automatic locking system to prevent any further problems like this one. I'll perform the usual protocol. Pass on the information to Murphy and shred the documents." The voice speaks once more to ask John a cleanup question. "That wasn't a problem it only cost three thousand to have the sheriff loose the file. His soon-to-be ex-wife wasn't too difficult I handed her the check for two hundred thousand and she signed the waiver removing the company from all liability." He pauses with the line coming through with his boss's opinion of the matter. "My plane is boarding sir. I'll check in with you tomorrow, bye." Returning the phone to his pocket he takes up his carry-on luggage with his right hand. Walking twenty steps he waits in line behind a young mother and her loud four year old daughter. Without needing to see her seating number he knows he'll be seated in front of them. *Just once it would be nice to take a flight without having to hear hours of crying.*

Redcap Asylum

D*ay One . . .*
"Hello Edgar, my name is Doctor Elizabeth Kelley. I've been asked to see you for the next few weeks to evaluate your mental state. Do you understand what I have just told you?" asks a young brunette woman in her mid-thirties wearing a white lab coat. Underneath her coat she wears a tan business pants suit. Sitting across the emplaced metal table is a man restrained in a cloth and a white leather-trimmed straight jacket. His black hair has been buzzed cut leaving only a short layer of fuzz covering the top of his perfectly circular melon. His face is frozen in an uncontrollable expression of fear.

"Yes," he replies in a solemn whisper. Through this entirely short interaction his eyes do not lift from the reflective surface of the metal table using short answers as a sign of his willingness to speak. Leaning to her right she thumbs through a large briefcase positioned beside her cloth-covered leg. The bag is filled with folders containing paperwork of various cases she is currently engaged in. Pulling out a tan folder with the label flap entitled *Edgar Stephens* she sets the bundle face up on the table. Reaching back into her bag she pulls out a digital audio recorder to position it to the center of the table along with pressing down the red record button. A small red LED light to the side turns on indicating the device is actively recording. Edgar looks at the recorder with a studious look of nervousness. Without pause he returns his eyes to look indirectly at the table top.

"If it's ok with you, Edgar, I'd like you to tell me your story?" she asks in an innocent none judging tone.

"Huh, my *story*," Edgar mimics back unpleasantly.

"I'm sorry, Edgar. Did I say something to offend you?" she asks with the same innocence in her voice.

"Well, yes, actually you did, Elizabeth," he snaps with his voice enraged. The level of his anger rises with each new word escaping passed his mouth. He starts thrashing violently back and forth against his unrelenting restraints followed by screams of terror inflicted by his inability to move. It's the all consuming fear many feel when faced with being physically restrained. Two large orderlies charge into the room followed closely by the so-called sympathetic warden. He looks to be a man who's spent much of his life standing face to face with all manner of criminal inmates. The warden is a man in his early forties, but his face appears aged far beyond those years. The top of his head has been shaved bald probably as a reaction to premature baldness. He does have a fully-formed black goatee speckled with gray hair throughout. The orderlies proceed to unhook the straps, which have held Edgar in place. The warden walks to the back of the chair where the mentally questionable Edgar Stephens has previously been restrained.

"I'm thinking the meeting is over for today," suggests the warden in a rhetorical tone. A condescending grin forms following this comment.

"I hope tomorrow will be more productive," Dr. Kelley states directly. Gathering her things she stuffs them into her bag. By the time she stands and heads for the room's exit the warden is holding open the door.

Day Two...

She's already set up at the table with her file and audio recorder in position when they bring in Edgar. Dr. Kelley is lines deep into an incident report filed late last night. The same two orderlies restrain him to the chair and exit to the other side of the interview room's door. For several minutes, they sit in silence for her to finish reading the full report. Edgar stares blankly at the surface of the table.

"I have in my hand the incident report telling of the events that transpired last night. I would like us to talk about it. Though first I would like you to tell me what happened on the night you were found standing over Katie's mutilated body," she asks followed by the report being placed on top of the open folder marked *Edgar Stephens.*

"What's the point none of you believe me," he comments in a downtrodden tone. "You all think I'm nuts."

"I don't have any opinion on that matter as of right now. I don't decide either way until I'm done with our meetings," she explains. Reluctantly he gives a surrendering sigh.

"I came home from a fourteen hour day at the scallop plant. I passed by her apartment door on my way to head up the last flight of stairs. I heard a gurgled scream from within her apartment. The door was shut, but unlocked I stepped inside to see what was wrong. As I entered the kitchen I saw her body lying there covered in blood. Her face was bashed in with unrelenting brutality. Worse than anything I've ever seen. Standing beside her was this goblin-looking creature. It must have stood about two to three feet tall. I watched in horror as it held its hat in its hand and begun to dip it into the pool of her dark crimson blood. The creature didn't stop until the hat was completely coated. Finally it noticed me; I must have startled it somehow, because it raced out of my sight to the left. I cautiously moved closer until I could see around the corner of the door. All I found there was a stone wall. I guess the creature must've disappeared into it, or through it, I'm not quite sure. I bent down to check if she still had a pulse, but she was long gone. She was probably already dead when I entered the apartment. Soon after the police came and found me there covered in her blood half-crazed by what I know I had seen. It was an easy case closed win. Now I'm in here trying to find anyone who will believe me before I die," he explains.

"This creature you're referring to is called a Redcap? Truthfully I had never heard of such a thing. I took the liberty to go online to look it up. I found that the Redcap originate from England and Scotland. They haunt ruined castles along the countries' borders. It's said they carry an iron pike and wear iron-shod boots. They attack travelers visiting these ruin castles and the only real way to escape is by reciting a verse from the Bible. Now, last time I checked the apartment building is definitely worn down, but not in ruin. We also live in America, not England or Scotland," she argues in an attempt to get him to either see the holes in his story or to see if he'll come up with reasons why it's still possible.

"That's easy to explain. This whole island the town is built upon used to be an old English outpost with numerous tunnels spanning from one end to the other. If you don't believe me go to the town hall and look up the town's history," he counters.

"How do you know this for sure," she asks still probing to see what comes out.

"My side hobby was in history. I love to explore the history of a family, a town, hell even of a building. Some of the things you'll learn by doing this will amaze you," he explains. Dr. Kelley notices his interest peak slightly before his true self sinks back below his guarded appearance.

"Ok to go back to your telling of the events. You said, when you came around the corner all you found was a stone wall. Where did the redcap go? He couldn't have just disappeared into the wall," she challenges.

"In truth, I haven't figured that part out for myself yet," he replies. From behind Edgar the interview room door opens and the two orderlies reappear. Removing the restraints from the table they walk him back to his room. The warden again holds the door open in wait for Dr. Kelley.

"Learn anything yet?" he asks tauntingly.

"Yes actually. But I could get a lot further along if I could keep him until I decide I'm done," she says with anger in her voice.

"A half hour a day is more than sufficient time to gather enough information to prove his insanity," he rebuts. Dr. Kelley pushes passed him to head to the main doors of the building. Leaving the facility she goes to the town hall and does as Edgar had instructed her. On researching the suggested history she finds all he said to be true. There are a total of twenty-three known tunnels intersecting throughout the island. Many of the tunnels still have the ruin remains of the fort's entrances accessible to enter down into the tunneled maze below ground.

Day Three . . .

Dr. Kelley enters the facility's doors and signs in on the visitor's guest book at the receptionist's counter. The nurse behind the counter hands Dr. Kelley another incident report this one dated from last night. Making her way down the labyrinth of corridors heading in the direction of the interview room she begins reading the report.

Edgar Stephens Incident Report May 14th, 1997 at 2:35 a.m.

The patient was screaming at an uncontrollable volume, thrashing and tossing the room's belongings (bed frame and mattress). The patient also was thrashing himself at the wall located on the left side of the room. When orderlies entered the patient had sustained minor cuts and gashes to both his hands and forehead (self-inflicted). The need of heavy sedation on the patient was called for due to the harm inflicted on his person. Further measures may need to be applied if the situation progresses further.

She is fully seated and ready to continue her routine examination with his file and audio recorder set on the table's surface when Edgar is brought into the room. She looks over his wounds closely to see if any bruising has occurred due to the orderlies' mistreatment. She makes the needed notes on his appearance and begins the session.

"Before we talk about what happened last night, I want you to know. I did as you suggested and went to the town hall to research the town history," she explains. Edgar looks up from the table to look her in the eye and then something she didn't expect happened he smiled.

"You did?" he asks in a genuinely uplifted tone. She nods and looks down to the two incident reports.

"Edgar in the last two nights, since beginning our meetings you have been having violent outbursts. Can you please explain to me what has been going on to make you lash out in these ways?" she asks in her same unintimidating tone. He returns his view back to the table and has a look of fear set upon his face. "What's wrong Edgar? You can talk to me. Maybe I can help, but you have to talk to me."

"It's followed me here," says Edgar in a low frightened voice a mere decibel over a silent whisper. "What I mean to say, is I've been moved to where it lives."

"What do you mean its home? Why does it live here out of all the places on this island of a town?" she asks wanting him elaborate on the answer.

"I don't know? All I know is I'm telling you what it told me two nights ago. It spoke to me through the wall on the left side of my room. It said it was coming for me, because I saw it. It taunts me all night driving me insane. Isn't that ironically funny, an inmate being driven insane in an insane asylum? Right before the sun began to rise through my window it said it will visit me for three days and on the fourth it will soak up my blood with its cap," he says with shaking fear hanging heavy with each syllable passing between his lips.

"But why four days?" she asks.

"That's how long it will take it to chip away at the wall to make an opening," he answers.

"Well that explains the first incident report. What about last night?" she probes.

"It has started to remove the white painted blocks of cement that make the walls of my room. It took away three blocks to show me the black nothingness that lies behind it. Out of the unnatural darkness I could see two horizontal oval red eyes watching me. It didn't say a word it doesn't have too. Its eyes torment me enough. The only sound I hear is the sound of the Redcap chipping away on the remaining blocks. I'm so scared. You have to get them to move me out of that room or in two more days they will find me dead," he pleads. Right on cue, the orderlies enter and take him back to his now torturous prison. The warden waits for her at the door as is his routine. Dr. Kelley walks passed him, but when he begins to speak she steps to his right.

"What would you say doctor, right off his rocker, huh?" asks the warden.

"I wouldn't know. I still haven't seen him long enough to forge any sort of opinion," she remarks. She returns to walk in her casual stride to the main doors. The warden walks along beside her to continue his conversation.

"Oh, come now quack. It's pretty obvious he's made up this whole Redcap story, because it's too frightening for him to admit he, himself, brutally bludgeoned the woman to a gurgling lump of blood-stained flesh. Everyone has the same opinion except for the celebrity-status seeking psychotherapist," he stabs. Stopping in her tracks Dr. Kelley turns her sights on the warden looking at him eye to eye.

"Would you have one of your orderlies check the bricks along the left wall of Edgar's room to see if any are loose?" she asks demandingly.

"Sure I'll have them check the wall just before they read him a story and tuck him under his blanket," he replies. She turns away to step out the exit after pushing in on the door's crossbar trigger.

Day Four...

Dr. Kelley walks into the facility and is greeted at the receptionist's counter by the warden. After signing in she is asked to follow him to his office for a chat. On entering the office he sits behind his desk of power, while she sits in a lone chair in the room's center. The space has a fairly warm feeling to it with everything set in a woodsy theme.

"What the hell are you doing in your meetings with my inmate, Doctor Kelley?" he demands.

"I'm finding out how he sees the important events that have transpired over these last few months," she returns. "I don't appreciate you questioning my procedures over evaluating MY patient, Warden. I've worked with half a dozen like-minded inmates and I have had successful diagnoses with each of them."

"I'm very aware of your distinguished career, Doctor Kelley. That's the only reason I've allowed you access to MY inmate. Ever since your arrival his nocturnal behavior has become increasingly violent over the last three nights," he explains.

"Three?" she questions.

"Oh yes, you haven't heard about last night," returns the warden. He pulls from an upper drawer to his right a pack of stapled papers and tosses them to the surface of the desk closest to Dr. Kelley. She quickly takes up the copy of the report and starts reading. "He carried on the same as he has the last two nights, but when the orderlies entered. Well, let's just say one of them is in the critical care ward of the town's local hospital. It took three hours to search the grounds and locate Mister Stephens and it took four orderlies to physically drag him back to his room. Once there they had to sedate him two doses above the usual amount just to calm him. The rest of the night he was restrained to his bed. All of this, because he thinks some mythical creature is after him chipping away at the bricks on the wall."

"Since he's having problems in that room I would respectfully request you move him to another room or even possibly another ward in the facility," she says in the calmest tone she can fathom to hold at this particular moment in time.

"Respectfully no, sorry, I'm not going to encourage his psychotic behavior like a problem-starting shrink that I've had the unfortunate displeasure to meet," he remarks. "Even if I wanted to oblige the mentally twisted in their derangement this facility is running at maximum capacity. There are no spare rooms."

"Can I see him?" she inquires.

"No. Well, not today at any rate. The high-level of sedation we administered needs more time to wear off," the warden explains plainly. On this answer Dr. Kelley rises from the chair to move to the door. Stopping with her hand on the handle she turns back to the warden. He sits in his chair holding the desk's phone to his ear.

"So, did your orderlies check the wall?" she questions.

"Yes, it's a perfectly solid BRICK wall," snaps the warden in reply.

Not wanting to quit the day, she returns to the town hall to check on the history of the building that now is the home for the criminally insane. Searching for nearly an hour before she finds far more then what she was looking for. She has not only found the reason why the redcap lives there, but when its life in America began. It had to have hidden dormant in the tunnels until time's natural decay had begun to reveal the scattered entrances all along the island. Whenever a new entrance is found the town officials order it to be sealed due to the potential dangers that would arise from people exploring within. Dr. Kelley also learns the building the asylum is housed in was in fact where the military leaders were barracked. It was the central hub for the island's whole tunnel network. The truly interesting bit is there were documents discovered from around this time, which shed light on incidents taking place of a very short creature stocking the tunnels. There were even reports of a few attacks. Military personnel were found bludgeoned to death and from the pool of blood surrounding the corpses tiny child-like footprints had been found disappearing into the tunnel's wall. Dr. Kelley returns home in desperate wait to bring this newly-found evidence to light. She stops mid-thought to pose to herself, *perhaps Edgar had also found these documents and he fed into the myth.*

Day Five...

Entering through the main door she stops at the sign-in counter. The attending nurse gives Dr. Kelley a concerning glance.

"The warden asked to be called the moment you arrive," she informs. "Will you sit over there, while I call him?" Dr. Kelley sits on the wooden bench to the right of the receptionist's station to await the warden's arrival.

"Doctor Kelley, I have some grave news to tell you. Will you please follow me? I'll explain on the way," he asks in a solemn tone. His face is longer, graver and paler than he has ever looked before to her. Though she's fairly certain as to what he's going to tell her, she goes along.

"I felt. Seeing as how he was the last few nights it would be prudent to take the precaution to strap Mister Stephens to his bed. Only after he began crying out did I order sedation. However, it seemed the sedative wasn't enough. Cause he still yelled through most of the night. Around three this morning he became abruptly quiet. All the orderlies had heard was of him pulling at his restraints followed by gurgled murmurs," explains the warden. They pass along various corridors of locked doors on their way toward the inmate ward.

"Ok. What happened when they checked in on him?" Dr. Kelley questions.

"Well. They checked in on him at six-thirty this morning --" he stops mid sentence while coming to a stop in the middle of the corridor. Without saying another word he points to the open cell door at the end of the hall. She holds her briefcase out for the warden to take. He does so without argument. Slowly Dr. Kelley walks toward the open door. She advances along the corridor with her legs feeling weighted down by pure stone. On looking within she sets her eyes on the grotesque lump of flesh, which was once the body of Edgar Stephens. She falls to her knees outside the small white room now coated in the darkest crimson any human could imagine. Once she regains her senses Dr. Kelley takes a couple of steps inside.

Edgar's body remains strapped to the bed. His face has been bludgeoned and horribly disfigured. Only half his teeth are going to be able to be used for identification. To the left of his bed a puddle of blood rests below what was once his face. The puddle has been smeared as if someone wiped something around in it. The next thing she notices makes her stomach turn and flush the color from her face. From the stirred puddle there is a pair of tiny bare footprints leading back to the wall to the door's left. The top half of the final footprint is cut off, due to the wall's cement brick firmly set in the way. Seeing this she quickly steps out of the room and turns to the warden.

"Warden, have you seen the footprints leading into the solid wall?" she asks. The warden nods his sickened face without even a sound escaping from his snow-colored lips. "They lead into the wall?"

"Maybe, some kind of prank to throw truth at his paranoia?" suggests the warden, whose still not wanting to admit the truth. Dr. Kelley takes her briefcase from him and momentarily digs inside hunting for the evidence to the truth he hopes to hide. Pulling out a yellow envelope filled with all she uncovered last night she pushes it against his chest forcing him to take the file.

"Maybe, this will convince you," she states. She walks passed him heading back the way she came.

"The police are going to want to speak with you," he calls to her from back down the hall.

"I'm sure they are, but they'll know where to find me," she answers. "Are you a religious man?"

"No?" he asks.

"Might want to learn a few Bible verses," she says. "They could save your life." She follows this farewell by turning down the intersecting hall on her way to the nearest church.

After the police ask their questions they leave. It's now nine-thirty at night and all Dr. Kelley wants to do is to slip into bed in hopes of forgetting the day's events, if only for a few hours. Lying on her back in her well-blanketed mattress she wiggles herself into her worn welcoming indent. With a relaxed sigh she closes her eyes and drifts off into her world of wonders.

The room gradually fills with the faint sound of something chipping away at stone. Its source originates from the wall of painted brick positioned to the left of her bedroom's half-bath doorway. The sound grows louder over the next few hours. The source has grown visible with each rhythmic chip. A block of brick roughly three feet above the floor shakes with each tap. The block looks ready to fall to the hardwood floor when she abruptly wakes into a sitting position between her blankets and mattress. She looks and listens for anything out of place in her dimly-lit room. Finding nothing at all she lies back into position and drifts off into the clouds once more.

From where the shaking brick was there is now a rectangular hole of darkness. Darkness darker than anything imaginable fills the space within. From out of this void appear two stubby blood-coated fingers. They grip along the edge of the brick below and from deeper within appears two horizontal oval red eyes. A voice breaks the room's silence in a raspy whisper, "*Four more days*".

Gasoline Burn Dream

Shriek the cries of the many long dead,
  that all flow to your head.
The dreams that haunt your every night,
from the bowels of your own hell they take flight.
Persisting the battle's lost.
Upon the scrolls the growling beasts roar,
to roam your soul and drown you whole.
The most gorgeous monsters come to life,
in the gasoline burn dream.
Trouble is bred by idle hands,
slap the cuffs so razored wrists are bound.
But the pain long since forgotten,
rises again from your inner fountain.
Trying to find the man that was.
For the body may be locked in a tomb,
but the soul will forever stay in this rubber room.

Marcelline

*I*ntruder

"Who are you? What are you doing in my house?" hollers a seventy-three year old widower into the unlit room before her. She points her late husband's double barrel twelve-gauge shotgun into the night-filled room. "I know you're here! I heard you bump against the table now show yourself!" Her eyes are old, but they are still in their prime. Holding her ground she firmly stares into the dark, like a cat readying to pounce on its unsuspecting prey. In the corner of her left eye she catches the faint glimpse. She shifts the barrels to the movement. With eyes fixed she waits for the intruder's next move. What had caught her eye begins to grow in clarity. It is a baby blue hoodie with some kind of Disney character on the front. Her mind isn't as acute as her eyes they are connected to, but soon she realizes the intruder is stepping forward into the light, towards her. She, in turn, takes a few slow steps back from the darkness. The intruder's clothes are fully visible with her facial features seeming to remain blurred, undefined. Accompanying the blue hoodie the intruder wears faded blue jeans and dirt-covered flat top shoes. She looks now to the face, which has cleared from its previously blurred state. The intruder has long straight chocolate brown hair with a petite nose resting in the middle of her face. Two bright blue eyes pierce the gap lying between the two females.

The only blue the old woman has ever seen that piercing was at the jewelry store on the day her husband bought her wedding ring. The blue jewel was sitting in a display case all alone. It was the largest gemstone she had seen. She was knocked breathless by the gem's beauty. She remembers thinking; *I'll probably never see a stone this beautiful or big again.* She's jolted back from her pleasant memory to the current one unfolding. The intruder now stands in the middle of the open archway allowing access between the dark living room and the well-lit kitchen. She finds with mouth-dropping disbelief her terrifying intruder is nothing more than a frightened young lady no older then sixteen. The old woman looks to the girl and lowers her gray brow into a scolding frown.

"What the hell are you doing in my house?" she questions. The young lady stares back with eyes stolen from a pouting puppy. "That won't work on me, child. Now answer my question." Her words are lies, because at this very moment her arms feel as if they are weighed down by eighty pounds of rock. She fights her subconscious to keep the gun pointed straight ahead. Right when her will is about to fail the girl speaks.

"It was cold and snowing . . . I had nowhere else to go," she answers in a whisper.

"Don't try my patience girl. It was a clear sky when I went to bed and the weatherman said it's supposed to be in the sixties the rest of the week. So, there can't possibly be snow outside," she replies. Her hard love routine isn't believable, but this girl is an unwelcomed guest at two-thirty in the morning. Protocol dictates the intruder should be spoken to only with an aggressively harsh tongue. In order to give the illusion to the victim of regaining some shred of their previous authority over their own domain after it was willfully trespassed upon. The fact still remains; the owner was caught with their pants down. She looks out the nearby window taking her eyes off the girl for a tenth of a second. The hibernating rose bushes out front of her kitchen window are coated in five inches of frosty white powder. She turns back to find her shotgun pointing into the empty darkness of the room ahead. The old woman looks out the front window to see the young girl walking with haste down the right side of the horizontal street passing along the front of her house. Lowering the shotgun she watches the girl walk away with her hood shielding her hair from the frozen rain cascading to the sidewalk. With the intruder having made her escape the old woman returns to her lonely chair stationed fixed beside the kitchen table and switches on the soothing sounds of the early morning ramblings of her local television.

The First Night

Two nights have passed since her keen senses caught the intruder in her living room. Its quarter to twelve by the time the old woman rinses and wipes out her empty coffee mug. She moves across the kitchen toward the dimly-lit hallway leading to the second floor staircase. After flipping the switch off to the kitchen light she stops midstep. Taking two steps back she peers out the front window as before she looks out into a snow-blowing night. Directly across the street in front of the seasonal bed and breakfast she sees the young girl sitting on the stone bench beside the BNB's stone and mason firepit. The firepit is used for the owners to give elaborate seafood cookouts for its out-of-state tourists staying during the summertime at the BNB. The girl sits upright with her legs folded in a fetal position. The woman's repressed mothering instinct takes control. Before she is fully aware of what her own body is doing she's opened the window and called to the young lady.

"Hey you get over here and come in out of this blizzard!" she hollers into the quiet night. Closing the window she makes her way to the locked front door. By the time she flips the screen door's latch the young lady is standing in wait to be allowed in.

They walk through the hall and into the kitchen where the woman switches back on the light hanging above the table. The old woman pulls out the first chair on the long side of the table and motions the girl to sit. The old woman grabs a metal kettle from beside the sink. Pulling up on the sink handle water pours into the kettle. Placing the kettle on one of the stovetop's burners she turns the appropriate knob to ignite the blue flame below. Opening the cabinet to her left she grabs a white mug decorated with pink flowers. Shuffling along the counter she reaches into the upper cabinet on the far right of the sink to remove two baby blue lettered packets. The kettle has begun to whistle. Grabbing the kettle she pours the scolding liquid into the mug and stirs the packets' contents into it. Walking with mug in hand she places it on the table ahead of the girl.

The girl stares at the mug intently. Watching the steam perform its beautiful ballet of vapors rising higher into the air until finally it vanishes. The girl wears the same clothes she had on the first night they met. The old woman eyes the fabric to see if any of it is wet and in need of cleaning.

"What's your name child?" she asks. Pulling out her wooden chair she sits to the girl's right. For a time the girl doesn't respond to her inquiry. "I'm sorry for pulling the gun on you the other night, but you scared the heck out of me." The girl lifts the warm mug to her lips and after a time lowers it back onto the table. "That's good, isn't it? Where's your home? Are you lost?"

"No, I'm not lost. I just don't have a place to call home anymore," she whispers.

"Well, what's your name?" repeats the old woman.

"Taurin," she answers.

"Taurin, that's a pretty name," she replies. "It is late and it's terribly unbearable out there. I have a spare room across the hall from mine. You can spend the night and tomorrow we'll figure out what to do with you." Taurin nods and starts to rise out of her chair. "Please finish your cocoa then we'll head upstairs." After three more mouthfuls the mug is set on the table empty. The pair head up the sturdy wood staircase to enter onto a large square hallway. There is one door directly to their left. When Taurin turns right she sees two more doors along the adjacent wall. The old woman guides Taurin along to the first door to their right. The door silently swings open to reveal a fully prepared twin mattress. "This is where you'll sleep tonight. I'll be across the hall if you need anything. The bathroom is downstairs. It's the first door to your left in the hall. Goodnight, Taurin."

"Thank you so much –" says Taurin stopping in the mid-sentence. "I'm sorry, but I still don't know your name?"

"Marcelline," replies the old woman.

"Goodnight, Marcelline," farewells Taurin. Marcelline closes the door behind her. She returns to her own queen-size mattress and crawls under her mountain of cozy blankets until she's woken at five-thirty by her bladder and need for coffee bean.

The Truth

The next morning, Marcelline sits on her round chair to the right of the kitchen table holding a cigarette between the fingers of her right hand. She lifts the steaming mug to her lips to take another sip from her freshly brewed coffee. Her eyes are locked onto the television as the meteorologist tells of the ferocious storm speeding towards Maine up along the coastline. New Jersey has already been buried in three feet of snow and it's only been twelve hours since the first snowflake. He also reports on the storm having claimed ten lives and snowbound thousands of others. This is the time she is joined in the familiar kitchen by a more comfortable looking Taurin.

"Are you hungry, Taurin?" she asks followed by her motioning with her left hand for the girl to once again sit in the same chair from last night.

"I'm fine," she answers, while sitting on the chair. Taurin looks over her right shoulder to see the picture on the television. A man is shouting about the great deals he has on the vehicles in his used car lot.

"If you'd like you can go in the living room and watch something else? I don't go in there much it was my husband's room. My room has always been the kitchen," explains Marcelline. She pulls a fresh cigarette from the rectangular white box and glows the tip. Her face is fogged over with an expression of smooth relaxation as the smoke fills her hungry lungs.

"How long have you smoked?" ask Taurin.

"Since I was twelve," she answers. Her reply is followed by a great and powerful coughing fit. After her fit has subsided she removes her hand from over her mouth to reveal numerous spots of speckled red dots on her palm. Taurin looks to her host with concern. "I'm fine --

I think. I had a series of test taken two weeks ago and Monday I have a follow-up." In an attempt to redirect the atmosphere Taurin continues her previous conversation.

"My dad used to smoke cigars," tells the young lady. Her voice is soft and choked with sadness.

"My husband used to smoke those as well," comments Marcelline accompanied with the same longing sadness. "Where are your mom and dad?" On the words releasing from her lips she fears the answer to come.

"They're gone," answers Taurin followed by a single tear running down her face. Marcelline grabs a tissue from the paper dispenser to her right, but she's distracted by the clanking of boots on the half deck behind her. A middle-aged woman with bushy bright red hair bursts through the door and begins to speak as soon as she removes her coat. At a quick glance she looks as though she's wearing a bouquet of blossomed roses on top of her head.

"Marcelline, you'll never guess who I heard is sleeping around with Mindy Strout," disrupts the unwanted guest. She crosses the kitchen to sit in the chair previously occupied by the now vanished Taurin. Marcelline looks around for any sign of the young lady.

"Where did she go? Did you see where she went?" she asks interrupting the new arrival. The loud-mouthed companion has to stop in the middle of her epic gossip to answer the question raised.

"Who?" she questions accompanied by a look of disgust for being interrupted.

"Taurin, the young girl, who was sitting in the chair before you burst in unannounced," answers Marcelline. Rising from her chair the old woman moves back to the doorway leading to the first floor hall. Reaching the top of the staircase she stops outside the spare room. She knocks three times before gradually opening the door. Looking around the room she sees no sign of the timid child. Her eyes fall on the twin mattress occupying the room. *Did she put things back exactly the way they were or did she sleep on the floor without using any of the bedding.* She closes the door on this sight and the accompanying thought.

After a short series of movements Marcelline rejoins the intrusive pest. "Taurin, where are you hiding? Please come out and join us." After a few seconds of nothing she returns to her seat.

"I think you've gone daffy. You were sitting here alone like always when I entered. By the way, I take offense to your irritation at my visit. From what I've seen no one else has stopped by to visit you lately. You'd do well to remember that!" snaps the offensively loud woman. She storms to the backdoor with coat in hand and leaves with a huffed snort.

Marcelline waits to make sure her quick departing guest doesn't intend to return. Once she's heard the woman's bass-vibrating Honda speed down the frozen asphalt she turns back to her coffee. In the middle of turning her sight locates the unmistakable eyes of Taurin. She's once more sitting in the seat to Marcelline's left. Marcelline jumps back into her chair from the sudden fright. She lands with a loud whispering creak from the chair. Instantly she sets her right hand over the middle of her upper chest and inhales four to six deep breathes. "Where did you run off to?"

"I don't like that lady," comments Taurin. She looks to the backdoor along the kitchen's back wall.

"I don't either, not really," Marcelline adds. "But she was around after Robert's death when no one else was. I guess I do owe her for that at least."

"If you don't mind my asking, how did he die?" asks Taurin in a low respectful tone.

"They said it was the stroke, but I know it was because he was simply tired," she explains to the attentive listener sitting upright in her chair. Marcelline can't place why, but she feels at ease with Taurin. The only other person she's ever felt this way for was Robert. Sipping her coffee she looks to the opposite end of the rectangular table where Robert's chair is positioned, unoccupied, and collecting dust. Her mind snaps suddenly reminding her to tell Taurin what she realized at five this morning. "Today is Sunday. The D.H.S. staff is closed until tomorrow. It looks like you'll have to stay here until then." Marcelline is glad of this fact, since she likes having another body staying under this roof. Rising from her chair she grabs the kettle again and fills it once more with water. She places it on an unlit burner. Turning the knob the burner ignites the spark containing a ring of short blue flames nestled around the center of the burner. The blue flames tickle the bottom of the kettle enticing the water inside to work itself into a frenzied boil. Stepping back to the table she grabs the mug from last night. Cold brown liquid spills over the rim to pass between the fingers of her wrinkled hand before falling in droplets to the linoleum floor. Looking into the cup her face grows into a dumbfounded expression. "Did you make your own cup when I wasn't looking?"

"No," replies Taurin. Her face has regressed back to a look of nervous sadness.

"I saw the cup last night it was empty. You had drunk it all," she states with confidence. Marcelline reminds herself of the sight of Taurin's room. Taurin looks to her as if reading her thoughts.

"Please sit down and I'll tell you the truth," she pleads. She gestures Marcelline to her chair the same way she had motioned Taurin last night. Their line of sight is broken by the kettle beginning to whistle. The old woman walks to the stove and turns off the burner. She immediately returns to her chair waiting for the fast-approaching truth.

Taurin straightens to sit upright looking to her attentive listener. Her face grows with increasing nervousness with hands fidgeting rapidly. She opens her mouth to speak, but nothing escapes. Taurin after a moment tries to control her mounting anxiety. "Promise me. You are not going to freak out when I tell you what I'm about to tell you."

"I can't promise that, but I'll try my best," replies Marcelline. Taurin takes a swallow before opening her mouth to speak.

"There's really no easy way to say this. So I'm going to come right out with it. I'm not really here; even though I am . . . I'm a ghost." Taurin says with a matter-of-fact tone. "I was raped and killed behind a row of thick bushes. I woke later that same night standing and looking down on my cold naked body lying on the ground. I stared for several minutes at myself. You can't imagine the shock I felt. I kept staring, watching for the slightest movement, but not even my chest would move." Marcelline listens to every word with eyes fixed on her storyteller. Her jaw muscles are beginning to hurt from physically forcing them to remain shut so not to further burden Taurin, who's spilling her heart-breaking story. "Finally after the ambulance hauled my body away I walked down the next three streets to get home to find a police officer telling my parents I died. My mother was crying, while my father fought hard to control his emotions. The next few years I stayed with them. In the beginning, I tried to communicate, but everything seemed only to upset them more. I was with them for five long years. By the end of those years they had moved on with their lives. Two years after my death my mother gave birth to my little sister. One day, standing in the kitchen my mother brushed passed me. She looked in my direction and broke into tears. She fell back onto one of the kitchen chairs. Through her sobs she spoke to me. *Why are you haunting me? Why won't you stop tormenting me?* It was then I realized they needed to move on, so did I." A period of silence hangs thick in the air, while Marcelline carefully thinks over what she's heard. *She is obviously alone and looking for companionship.* Looking into Taurin's piercing eyes she is lost within them.

"How long have you been on your own?" The old woman asks.

"I left my parent's home in the early part of nineteen ninety-two, I think or maybe it was earlier," answers Taurin.

"You've been on your own for eighteen years!" exclaims the old woman. "It's settled! You are staying here with me. You need the same thing I need, companionship. We're two drifting souls gliding through time waiting for who knows what." Taurin's frowned disposition shifts in a blink into a mind-bending smile.

"Really, you mean it?" she returns excitedly. Marcelline smiles at Taurin's reaction to her suggestion. The two new companions sit the rest of the day locked in the cozy kitchen telling each other their experiences in both life and death. "I've been to Paris, London, Tokyo, Australia -- I spent a year there -- that's my favorite place. I even saw the pyramids in Egypt. My whole short life I always wanted to see the pyramids, but when I visited them as a spirit all I could feel was the misery of the ones buried within. I wouldn't suggest seeing them after you've passed on."

"You've lived more after death then most who live to be a hundred," comments Marcelline.

"I have to admit, no matter where I went following my death I always wanted to go home to see them," remarks Taurin solemnly. "That's why I've spent the last several years in this town."

"Only natural, in the whole world there's no place that can replace the warm feeling you feel on returning home," she says in an attempt to comfort the distraught specter. Marcelline looks to the snow-fuzzed darkness outside her kitchen window, which shrouds this island of fisherman and their families. Turning to look over her left shoulder she reads the clock. Marcelline doesn't have to squint like her peers to see the position of the hands, two thirty-five a.m. "It's late. I better get my butt to bed. I have my appointment tomorrow afternoon. I'll see you in a few hours, goodnight." The old woman walks up the staircase to the second floor. Upon the sound of the door connecting to the wood frame Taurin begins her short hours of solitude once more.

The Discovery

Five hours of silence is broken by the turning of the bedroom doorknob followed by the unevenly spaced creaks of the old woman's footsteps coming down the staircase. The first thing to be done is make a quick stop at the bathroom. Entering the kitchen Taurin turns to her with a greeting grin.

"How'd you sleep?" she asks.

"Fine, but I'm having problems breathing when I lay down. That's why I have an appointment today," replies Marcelline. Walking over to the automatic coffee maker she removes the pot of freshly-brewed black coffee. Grabbing up her washed mug she pours a cup of the muck. Turning to Taurin she closes the distance to the table and her unoccupied chair. The two new friends sit in silence for several minutes. Only after she refills her second cup does Marcelline break the silence.

"Did you sit there all night?" she asks on returning a second time to her chair with the mug gripped tightly in her hand. Taurin gives a nodded reply. "I should have stayed up I had such a rough night. All I could hear through the silence was a continuous ding sound."

"I didn't hear anything," adds Taurin. Her statement is followed by an expression of mixed emotion, of concealment. Marcelline has a shiver crawl up her spine from the girl's physical reaction. She looks to her companion with a puzzled glance. "What?"

"Nothing," answers the old woman following a few more minutes of silent contemplation. "Well, I have to get dressed now or I'll be late." Marcelline rises from her chair to head upstairs to change out of her home attire. Fifteen minutes pass quietly before Taurin hears returning footsteps descending the stairs. The old woman enters back through the doorway into the kitchen. Passing Taurin she stops at the coat rack to the right of the backdoor. Marcelline throws her over-sized green and gray winter coat. "I'll be back in a few hours. You can watch television if you'd like to help pass the time." Marcelline turns the brass doorknob, opening the door. In a blink she's on the other side of the door heading to her gray station wagon.

Minutes transform into hours. Hours accumulate like coins in the taxman's satchel. Taurin's quiet kitchen is disrupted by the rumble of an engine and a flash of headlights through the kitchen's side window. She aims her excited eyes to the wall clock to see its now four forty-five. Minutes later a worn out looking Marcelline enters through the backdoor. After hanging up her coat she grabs the pot of hours old coffee to pour her mug two-thirds full before scooting her feet across the floor to her chair. Taurin is unable to hide her nervousness and slouches silently in her seat. Taurin keeps a keen eye on the sadness-stricken woman, who she's quickly come to call friend.

"What's wrong?" she asks breaking the silence. Marcelline stares at an object on the table's surface. She may be looking at the object, but her thoughts are light years away. "Marcelline?" The old woman snaps back to the present to look up at Taurin with a shocked gaze.

"I have cancer," she states with a hollow voice. Her face is vacant like her mind, while she tries to process the newly-acquired information. "The test results came back late Friday. It's advanced. They are giving me two months."

"What can you do?" asks Taurin in honest concern.

"They're talking about chemotherapy. The hope is it will freeze the cancer from spreading any further," she explains. Her emotionless expression breaks into uncontrollable tears. Taurin wants to put her arm around her, but she can't no matter how hard she may want to. "I'm sorry, I'm going to bed. I'll see you in the morning." Marcelline makes her way up the staircase to her room. On the sound of the door closing Taurin once more is left alone in the lit kitchen.

The Bells

The hours pass until the sun rises from its dark sheets to illuminate the cloud-filled sky. No sound is heard in the house, except for a slightly louder dinging whisper hovering in the air. Taurin waits in her chair. Eyes positioned on the muted people moving in the lighted box on an unfinished wooden shelf. The clouds mixed with the sun's rays fill the kitchen in a grayish blue haze. The warm feel of the house has vanished replaced by a melancholy and sickly suffocation. This feeling is all too familiar to Taurin. It's the feeling of looming death. This self-contained thought is broken by the turning of the upstairs doorknob. Marcelline descends the staircase quickly and in a blink she's standing beside Taurin.

"What is that sound I know you hear it too?" questions Marcelline. Taurin can see the old woman's confusion at what is going on with her. "I began to hear it the night you came into my house. Now tell me the truth about what's going on?" The old woman steps around Taurin's chair to reach her own. Taurin's face shifts to her worried expression, because she knows Marcelline won't like the answer.

"Yes, I can hear it too. I first heard the sound, while I lay helpless and bruised upon my grassy deathbed. It's the sound hailing the coming arrival of creeping death, the tolling bells," Taurin explains. "The sound will gradually grow the closer you get to your time," Sadness fills her eyes. She sits helpless watching her living friend's mind struggle to process this information.

"For whom the bell tolls," Marcelline whispers. Looking up she sees Taurin staring back. "That is what I had thought." She pulls a cigarette from the white pack to her right. Lighting the tip she slowly inhales causing the tobacco on the tip to glow orange. After holding the smoke in her lungs for a short time she exhales sending a smoky white puff into the air. The two companions watch the ball of smoke rise to the ceiling. Halfway up the ball spreads and begins to separate. The last remnants of the smoke collide into the cross beam of the ceiling. It ripples and glides three-sixty from the point of impact. "That puff of smoke is a lot like a human life." Taurin turns her view to Marcelline not sure what she's driving at. "It travels along its course; sure, pieces have chipped away on its rise. Then when the smoke reaches its end it smashes into oblivion." She takes another puff and again watches it rise to its unavoidable destruction. Taurin is nervous by the coming silence growing; however she is also just as nervous to speak out.

"Chemo might be able to prolong your life," she says. "The bells are still very faint. Death has yet to show itself." She's not sure if anything she has just said sunk into Marcelline. She puffs smoke and watches it collide above her head. Taurin spends the remainder of the day sitting in the kitchen with her friend basking in silence's embrace.

The Doctors' Treachery

Five years have passed since her diagnosis of cancer. Taurin sits in the kitchen waiting for Marcelline to enter through the backdoor. Opening the door, she steps inside trailed by the windblown snow. Shrugging off the cold Marcelline peels out from under her weather protection. Pouring a fresh mug of mud she joins Taurin at the table.

"How'd the appointment go?" she asks. The old woman sips from her cup in silence enjoying the hot liquid gliding along her throat.

"They say the cancer has begun to grow. The chemo has stopped working," she explains.

"What are they going to do to stop it?" Taurin probes.

"Nothing. They forced this. They have a new experimental treatment they want me to give them permission to try," replies Marcelline.

"If they think it will work shouldn't you try it," she suggests.

"You don't understand," Marcelline says with a growl to her words. "They cut back on the chemo the last several treatments to allow it to happen. They've killed me." Her wrinkled face shows her disgust over their actions. Taurin doesn't utter a word she simply waits. The silence builds thick in the gradually confining kitchen.

"So what are you going to do?" Taurin asks in an attempt to understand what's on her companion's mind.

"I really don't know. I'm so tired. Maybe I should except the fate laid out before me. I've had five bonus years and I've long since prepared myself for death," she says in a tone sounding more like outward thinking than a conversation. Not much else is said on the subject for the rest of the day. They spend the day, as usual, in the kitchen watching the active people on the television. The house fills with saddened misery like it did all those years ago. Taurin knew this was coming, knew the cancer had started to grow. Returning to claim what was stolen for so many years. It was the bells that told her. Over the last few weeks the sound had started too grown once again.

Death's Arrival

Two weeks have passed since the murderous confession of Marcelline's so-called doctors. She's withered down to eighty-nine pounds. Her days and nights have become filled by fits of constant coughing. Taurin sits in the corner of Marcelline's room, while the nurse checks on her and helps with her physical needs. Once they're alone Taurin will sits on the bed to the right of her fading companion. Their talks have become graver and have become more of one's belonging to a mother and her daughter.

"Next to my Robert, you are the best friend I've ever had," confesses Marcelline between spasms of throat–shredding coughs.

"And you're mine. A sad state of affairs, isn't it? I find my best friend on her approach to the grave and you find yours decades after she's stopped breathing," comments Taurin. The statement is followed by the two of them joining in a short chuckle. It is short lived as another coughing fit kicks up. Taurin looks to the old woman's hollow shell with sad realization over the fact she'll soon be alone again.

Even with the nurses staying at the house the inevitable will come to pass. Under protest Marcelline is moved to the Calais hospital. The bells ring so loud it's as if they are right beside Taurin's ears. She knows Marcelline hear them too, but doesn't show any signs of it bothering her. The pain must be distracting her focus from off them.

Taurin sits in an ugly orange chair several feet from Marcelline's bedside. It's a two-bed suite with the second bed remaining unoccupied, since its last occupant departed soon after Marcelline arrived. She's fast asleep for the moment. Apparently the morphine is doing its job. Taurin watches her with mixed emotions. On the one hand she's sad at her approaching departure. She's also jealous at where she'll likely be heading. Looking up from the bed Taurin sees a figure standing in the room's doorway. The figure's eyes glance across the room at Taurin. It takes a single second for her to know this stranger to be Death. It stands six foot five. A long black cloak covers its scrawny skeletal frame. The fiery red hair is cut short. Its face is perfectly circular, but in some ways flat. The eyes are small and pierce with something not quite natural. Its lips appear to change in a constantly shifting manner. Taurin shivers upon first glance. This is not Death's natural appearance, only camouflage.

"You are here for her aren't you?" she asks. Death stands motionless and tilts its gaze to the slumbering cancer victim. It turns back to the intruding specter. The disguised figure gives a questioning stare as to her presence.

"Can't you hear the bellsss? Her time hasss been a long time coming, but now it'sss upon usss," comments Death. Taurin sheds the shadow of a tear down her left cheek.

"How much longer does she have?" she probes further.

"None. Timesss up," it answers.

"Can I have a few minutes to say goodbye?" she pleads. Death stares vacantly at her not saying a word. After a few seconds the figure nods in a graceful motion. The figure stays in the doorway giving the dead and soon-to-be a private moment alone. Death has never understood nor taken a liking to mankind's mushy emotions. To Death emotion is an annoying complication. "Before you go can I ask a question?" the dark figure looks back to this lost soul.

"Be quick. Your time hasss already begun," Death remarks.

"When I died. Why didn't you come for me?" she asks. The figure for a time only stares blankly. Its lips continue to slightly change in size and now she has taken to notice other oddities of his appearance. There are no eyebrows and what is stranger still no eyelids.

"You're what the Almighty callsss a moral missstake. When each life isss created their ssstatusss isss neutral, ssstuck center 'tween good and evil. There are thossse sssoulsss who have managed to ssstay centered 'tween the two posssitionsss and therefore have no place in Heaven nor Hell. They are simply left to roam thisss sssspiraling ball until it'sss end."

"I'm a mistake," remarks Taurin. Death stands in silence with only its eyes giving over to its awareness of the room. Taurin sits in the chair with Death's words repeating in her head. She stares until the dying woman speaks.

"Don't be upset it'll soon be over and I'll help you to Heaven. Where you belong," comforts Marcelline. Her voice is weak and strained, sounding as if the words are forced by a wisp of air. On these last words her body and spirit part. Marcelline finds herself seconds later standing beside her hallow shell. Her eyes spread wide upon looking down at her shrunken body. Marcelline shifts her view to her saddened friend. She walks through the bed to stand beside Taurin. "Are you ready to go?" From behind her a bright warm glow shines down over her, encapsulating her within its warmth. The dark form of Death stands in wait for Marcelline's ascension. Grabbing Taurin's hand the old woman pulls her into the light. Upon entering Heaven's glow Taurin is struck by extreme pain from an unimaginable heat.

"I can't go with you. It's meant for only one soul and that one soul is you. Go, be with your husband. I'll be fine," pleads Taurin. She pulls back from Marcelline with another shadow of a tear running along her cheek. Turning her back to the center of the room she walks through the wall. Stepping onto the freshly cut grass of the hospital's front lawn. She stops twenty feet from the hospital wall and waits. A couple of endless minutes pass by before she feels the warmth of Heaven vanish. The only joy she feels is the silence from the tolling bells. The only bells she hears now are mere whispers compared to those of Marcelline's. Taurin walks slow with her thoughts remembering the last five years of joyful memories. Her thoughts are jolted by a hand resting on her right shoulder. Turning she looks into the familiar eyes of Marcelline.

"I was thinking ever since I was a kid. I've always wanted to visit Ireland. How about it?" asks Marcelline. Taurin's face brightens into a great smile.

"You know, I don't think I've been there," she replies. The two friends continue across the field. "Why didn't you go and be with you husband?" Marcelline shakes her head.

"If Robert was to have found out I left you here I'd never have heard the end of it," she answers with a chuckle. "Heaven can wait. Besides, we have all of eternity to find a way for you to join us on that white cloud."

Plague of Consequence

The plague spread affecting any in its presence. Those who escaped locked themselves within walls made of wood and stone. Those touched by the plague were deemed as lepers. Like lepers they were cast aside by any and all who could help or grant sympathetic reason. They were made to become disfigured with hunched backs by the early stages of the plague. Many died within weeks at the start of the affliction's later stage. This plague was not fatal, a strange fact too late to save many. Then how did they die you ask? Though many tried to give it reason, I know why. Each and everyone died of a broken heart set forth by their abandonment to the dark, giving up on life, itself. Their families - their lives tossed them out. Once abandoned and cold they took to crawl into dark alleyways giving up their lives as forfeit.

Alone they did die. For as disfigured as they were they still retained their biased minds. As one would look onto the other they disgusted one another. This desperate loneliness could have been thwarted. If not for what they were taught lead to their lonely thoughts.

This plague has claimed far too many in this town. Many townsfolk understood just how close they came to the very precipice of Hell's jagged edge. Many a heart-torn action had befallen these very townsfolk. For parents of many had cast aside their children of youth, just as these same parents years prior cast asunder their elderly parents of old. For fear crept within the town's very veins forcing all to cast aside that, which they once loved and cared for, this plague having squeezed to a stop the very growth of this once great town's future hope.

Left did the plague just as instantaneously as its ravaged force spewed forth across the town. The townsfolk did rejoice by this new-found breath at life and with mournful hearts heaved by recent past transgressions pushed ever onward. In time, the town bloomed anew towards their future's assured hope. The parents of youth and loss began to rekindle new offspring once more. These parents who had cast aside their parents of old, over time, did too became parents of old. This one-time plague of the past they did bury deep and coat with ample lime. A town's dirty secret never to be retold.

One sunny day in the later part of May came the resurgence of the town's past secret carried forth on the winds of the day. Took the parents now old only a short breath of life to recognize this one-time plague had returned. The plague spread through the streets infecting all for whom it touched. Like before the town could have split into two, those uninfected, those rejected. However, times having changed so too had the minds and souls of the parents of youth. These new parents of youth gave over to protect their offspring. Fear had not simply cast aside the afflicted to the dark, to die alone. Through this change of heart these children of youth fought their disfigurations, to survive this plague of old. The children of youth surely will pass through to reach their age of old.

Neither had the children of old cast out their elderly parents when fear did creep within their veins. These parents of old did become plagued by their forgotten thoughts to dark actions manifested. For they had cast them out upon the cold cruel streets their children of youth when fear did burrow deep to lay sickness within their hearts.

These same parents now elderly grew to fear for their forsaken fate. They come to feel the agony of their children of youth keeping around them. The abandon's retribution is at hand. These parents of youth - now old, speak to tell their children of now to what atrocities had feverishly commenced upon their forgotten brethren. One by one, these guilt-ridden parents of old died within their cloth tombs.

With the last of the old beginning to fade he spoke on seeing his child of youth standing before the foot of his bed. Her arms outstretched beckoning him to come hither. His final words did send shivers through his children of now. "I'm so sorry."

The plague of old has never since been seen to return. This plague, like a spirit of unresolved grief appears fulfilled by what has since been finished. This plague crept within this town twice over. Once forgotten, this forgotten hardship shall surely again return giving to question the townsfolk as to the cost of regaining one's own innocence.

The End to the Beginning

1. "Wilhelm Gilroy, the one who found the signal?" asks a gray haired general in a green military uniform. The general directs his question to a man, who looks more like a football player, then a computer nerd who listens to airwaves waiting on messages from alien life.

"That's me, sir. But why have you brought me here?" Wilhelm asks. The general glares directly into his eyes not saying a word. With relief to Wilhelm the military man begins to explain.

"That transmission you decoded is a blueprint for a communication device from an unknown alien lifeform," he gives a moment's pause for effect. "The device has been built and sent to our orbiting military space station positioned over Mars."

"That's great, sir, but I still don't understand what this has to do with me?" asks Wilhelm, while he stands facing the general.

"Last week we received another transmission demanding first contact be made by the one who discovered the transmission," he reluctantly reveals with a tone of disgust.

"Why? I'm just a computer geek who got lucky. I'm no goodwill ambassador," he counters.

"That maybe. You are what they asked for so you are what they're going to get. The shuttle will take you to the station in ten minutes," explains the general. He shows Wilhelm to the oak double door located directly behind him. They proceed along a marble-floored hallway.

"If you don't mind my asking why make contact with us now?" probes Wilhelm, while turning to look to the general on his right.

"I posed that very same question to the eggheads back in Washington. They're under the opinion it has to do with Dylan Murphy's antimatter drive system," he answers without shifting his gaze from the far end of the hall. They reach the glass door with the general stopping midstep to face Wilhelm again. "One more thing, as I said earlier it is a military station. Run by Colonel Telley, a hard-nosed pain in the ass, though trust me if the shit hits the fan he's the man you want in your corner. My point is even though it is his facility we're placing all authority of the alien technology in your hands, Mister Gilroy. If at any point you feel you or anyone else's life is in danger hand over control to Colonel Telley." On finishing this statement he extends his right hand and waits for Wilhelm's.

"Understood General," he replies, at the same time he takes hold of the general's offered hand. With farewells exchanged Wilhelm pushes passed the glass door to be escorted to the MP's jeep.

The small shuttle ascends into the sky by two massive thrusters located to the sides of the craft. Once the shuttle reaches the upper atmosphere the pilot switches on the antimatter drive and they blast into the darkness in the direction of the orbiting station located over Mar's settlers' encampment.

"We should reach the station in one hour," reports the pilot. Wilhelm nods from his seat to the pilot's right. He looks out the window at the non-changing backdrop of stars speckled across the blackness of space. An hour has passes by before the pilot breaks the silence occupying the shuttle's interior. "We will be docking in three minutes, Mr. Gilroy." Once the craft is docked in the bay the back hatch opens allowing its passengers to exit. Wilhelm rises to his feet as Colonel Telley enters the shuttle.

"Wilhelm Gilroy?" asks the colonel in a thick southern drawl.

"Yes Colonel, sir," he answers respectfully.

"Follow me to my office we have matters to discuss," orders the colonel followed by him stepping back out through the shuttle's open door. Wilhelm trails behind him exiting the shuttle. They make their way down corridors of white with various plants strategically spread along them. *These halls look exactly like the ones back at the military compound on Earth. If it wasn't for the occasional passing window revealing the blankness of space I'd swear I was still there,* comments his inner voice. Entering through a doorway, the pair of men occupies an office covered by wall-sized screens imitating a wooded landscape with the occasional critter scampering by. Wilhelm shuts the door behind him. The colonel cozies onto the high-backed leather desk chair. He signals with his right hand for his guest to take a seat on one of the chairs positioned in front of his desk.

"I know why you're here, but in my opinion it's the biggest mistake we've made since pulling out of Vietnam. We have enough damn enemies back on Earth. The last thing we need are more with unknown weapon capabilities. I want you to report to me on everything that happens in these talks you'll be having with the E.T.'s," asserts the colonel with a firm scowl set to intimidate Wilhelm.

"I was told I had complete control over this assignment. Being this is not strictly a military operation," replies Wilhelm flatly. Colonel Telley's face hardens with a reddish glow from a sudden twinge of anger held under his collar.

"If contacting alien life is not a military exercise, what the hell is?" he snaps with a scoff.

"I don't know what to tell you. I'm only repeating the parameters I was given by the general. I may have no military background, but last time I checked a general holds the higher rank, Colonel Telley. The general told me that –" Wilhelm's argument is cut short, due to the colonel interrupting.

"Save me your orders," he barks with an aggressive growl. "I was also briefed on the original parameters of this exercise. I'm altering it."

"I am truly sorry colonel. My orders are specific. I'm not to hand over control to you, unless, the situation becomes hostile. It hasn't, so I'm still in control, sir," says Wilhelm reaffirming his stance in a desperate fighting to hold his ground against Colonel Telley.

"Fine, for now," he surrenders with a cynical chuckle. A wave of his hand signals the conversation is at an end and Wilhelm can leave his sight. "The private outside will take you to your quarters." Wilhelm rises from his chair to step through the door and back into the hall to the waiting private. To Wilhelm the young private looks as though he's just started shaving.

2.

After Wilhelm gets some nervous sleep and changes into the blue jumpsuit accompanied with his personnel I.D. card with a level seven clearance he steps out of his room. He's escorted by the same young private to an empty white room filled by an oversized bizarre-looking machine. Seconds later, Wilhelm is joined by a dark-skinned man draped in a white lab coat.

"Are you ready for a trip, pal?" the man asks in a tone with no real defined emotion.

"Will it hurt?" asks Wilhelm. He looks nervously at the machine.

"No . . . well it's not supposed too," answers the man. "You see, what this machine will do is remove your living entity from your body and send you to a gaseous planet that's already been prepped as a relay station, of sorts, for us to establish communications with the alien race."

"Entity?" questions Wilhelm with his heighten feeling of anxiety doubled.

"You can call it your spirit, soul, or even life-force. Though before you ask, which I know you're going to I don't know where this planet is. We do know it's not in our solar system," replies the lab tech in further explanation.

"What do I need to do?" he asks. His view swings from the machine to the tech.

"Nothing, just stand here while I strap you in," replies the lab tech. Wilhelm steps back to stand upright against a metal slab. The tech proceeds to strap Wilhelm into the locking restraints. The tech secures Wilhelm's arms, legs, and waist. The tech straps a strange contraption on top of Wilhelm's head. "The headpiece's wires will synch you to the machine."

"You sure this won't hurt?" asks Wilhelm nervously.

"Definitely. Won't hurt a bit," replies the tech, while walking across the room to stand beside the controls. "Or it will hurt like hell. We don't know yet, but we are keen to find out." The tech flips a few buttons causing the machine to come to life with a high-pitched vibrating hum. It's not the usual kind of mechanical hum heard back on Earth. The hum is of a rolling set of particular pitches. The tech looks to Wilhelm. "Ready?" The tech's finger hangs over a large black switch.

"Ready as I'm going to be," he replies with a face of complete unease.

"That a boy," remarks the tech. The instant the man flips the switch Wilhelm feels a rushing blast, like thousands upon thousands of watts of electricity is coursing through every vein at the speed of light. The overall feel of this sensation is one of a chilled numbness pulsating through him. Wilhelm's body thrashes furiously as his mouth froths with thick white foam. Following a few moments of this action his body relaxes to dangle motionlessly with his chin falling upon his chest. The lab tech checks Wilhelm's vitals to find he's breathing along with a normal pulse rate. The tech bridges the gap to the intercom along the adjacent wall across the room. Holding in the red button he speaks into the microphone.

"Colonel. It's working fine, sir," he says into the receiver.

"Good son, report back if any changes occur," orders Colonel Telley's voice from out of the speaker.

"Yes, sir," replies the tech. He returns to monitoring Wilhelm's vitals and the machine's diagnostic systems.

Wilhelm floats in what appears to be white vapor. Every inch around him is filled with this fog-like vapor. It's as though he's standing in the middle of a cloud. His visibility is less than tolerable, but he can see his hands. In fact he can see his whole body. He is giving off a light blue glow, which illuminates the foggy vapor of this gaseous planet. Through the fog he begins to see another faint light source in a green glow from what he assumes to be the alien being coming to join him. On seeing the being's form he thinks to himself, *it's not like I'd thought it would be. It looks so human, except its limbs are insanely stretched. Its long neck must stretch three to four times our own and its arms and legs are doubled. It's has no distinctive features. No eyes, nose, mouth, or ears to speak of. It stands free from clothing. The only way I can describe it is to say it's of solid light, a freestanding green glowing silhouette.* The being comes to a stop ten feet from Wilhelm. The first few minutes they stand motionless facing one another with anxious silence engulfing Wilhelm's most intrusive thoughts.

"My name is too much for your primitive mind so you may call me Glandda," the being says breaking the silence. Wilhelm takes a moment to realize it's speaking to him telepathically. The being acts as though it knows what he's thinking, because it gives him a slight nod as to assure his hypothesis is accurate.

"You're a lot smarter than my fellow companions thought you to be," states Glandda with a voice cold and unemotional. "Although your race remains to be quite primitive." Glandda's face does not make any expressions, while its body's movement stands fixed. "On your previous thought as to my form." The being gives a slight pause as though searching for the appropriate words. "My race, as you would say has cast aside our physical form and evolved into beings of a formless entity. As to my present form set before you now it's one the system felt would put you best at ease."

"Are there a lot of your kind?" he asks.

"There are far too many to count," replies the being.

"Strange to think you speak English several galaxies away," he thinks without thinking.

"The device we're using translates the other's thoughts so it is understandable. In actuality, our normal thought waves would make your mind implode from our advanced evolution," corrects Glandda with an undertone of superiority.

"Where does your race come from and is that where you're communicating from?" he continues to probe in an attempt to learn as much as he can from their first meeting.

"Your race is, as you would say -- a very inquisitive one," declares Glandda in an annoyed tone. "My races' planet has long since been destroyed. My kind now inhabits a lifeless planet five galaxies from yours. It has no name for we have no desire to name a floating rock in space. Your race has mastered what you call antimatter. In this line of thought your race must have already mastered what you'd call nuclear fusion, yes?" Glandda's question is almost spoken in a rhetorical tone.

"Yes, we've mastered nuclear fusion. Why'd you want to know a thing like that for?" he responds. Glandda pulls from out of Wilhelm's sight a device and holds it in its elongated right hand. The being proceeds to aim the small spherical device toward Wilhelm. He attempts in a nervous way to change the subject. "Is there anything else you'd wish to learn about my race or our planet?"

"That won't be necessary," returns Glandda accompanied by Wilhelm's puzzled gaze. "You see as we've been talking I have collected all the knowledge from your mind. I now know all you know. I find it puzzling your race can function with having such a limited space to store one's knowledge."

"Then why call for this meeting if not to share mutually beneficial knowledge?" he asks. Glandda doesn't answer the question. "Why the question about nuclear fusion if you already knew everything I know?" A sickening feeling creeps through and into the pit of his stomach.

"I had to direct your mind to those series of thoughts to be sure I could successfully retrieve the wanted information," it answers. "Your planet needs nuclear fusion capabilities to sustain us."

"Sustain?" repeats Wilhelm nervously.

"I want to show you something," comments Glandda as it raises its arm stretching out toward Wilhelm. A great green glow begins building at the spherical tool's tip.

"What does that device do?" he asks, while trying to see passed the ever building ball of light.

"You'll soon find out," replies Glandda.

Meanwhile, back in the lab where Wilhelm is strapped to the upright metal slab. The lab tech sits monitoring his vitals. His work is again interrupted by Colonel Telley calling to demand a progress report on Wilhelm's status.

"Any change?" asks the colonel's voice from out of the speaker.

"No sir. I told you before everything checks out," answers the tech. Without warning, Wilhelm screams in excruciating agony as though his limbs were being torn apart at their joints. Moments later, his heartbeat stops registering on the colored monitor. The lab tech is shocked with adrenaline, due to this unexpected development. He springs into action pressing a large red button on the monitoring station. Leaning forward into the microphone of the communication system he calls emergency personnel. "I need a medical team to lab fifty-one immediately -- repeat -- I need a medical team in lab fifty-one immediately." Seconds pass before a medical team bursts through the lab door. Removing Wilhelm from the restraints they lay him on the ground. One of the medics begins to apply CPR.

"Paddles half power -- clear! Not working, alright full-power -- clear!" calls the medic each time she sets the electrical paddles against Wilhelm's chest. It's a futile effort ending in pronouncing Wilhelm Gilroy dead at 18:54. The medics place him in a black body bag followed by the same two medics gathering their scattered used supplies. The female medic is reaching over the bag to grab one of her tools when without warning the bag lunges upright scaring her into almost having a minor heart attack. The body in the bag sits upright. The female medic unzips the bag to look face to face with Wilhelm's open eyes.

"Who are you and why am I in a bag?" he asks. This question catches the attention of both of the remaining two people in the lab. The tech comes over to where Wilhelm sits on the ground still half covered by the body bag.

"You've been dead for twenty minutes," answers the tech in a shocked tone.

"Twenty minutes -- that is a long time," states Wilhelm in no particular tone of shock. In fact, he shows no emotion to speak of, except for a grin cemented to his face. Colonel Telley enters through the lab door as the medic helps Wilhelm out of the black bag.

"Sir, look at Mister Gilroy. He's alive! He was dead for twenty minutes, but now he's back," says the tech in a state of hyper excitement. Telley looks to Wilhelm with a somber expression. "He says he feels fine, which the medic corroborates. He said the aliens told him, due to our race's anatomy he may suffer some side effects when first he tries to reunite his entity back within his physical shelf. Guess it would depend on the entity's body type if it would need to restart, if you will. Basically that is what seems to have happened to him. His whole body's system had to shut down before it could return to peak operating capacity." Telley examines Wilhelm from a good distance. Eventually he turns his attention to the lab tech.

"I want a detailed report on everything that transpired in this room for the last hour and a half on my desk by tomorrow morning?" orders the colonel in a rhetorical question. The tech nods in acceptance to the order and leaves the room.

"What happened out there, Wilhelm?" questions Colonel Telley firmly. Wilhelm deliberately ignores the question. With his anger rising he grabs hold of Wilhelm's shoulder to forcefully direct his attention. "Answer me you little pissant!" One thing the colonel can't stand is the lack of respect his rank receives from any no-account civilian.

"Sorry, what was the question?" he returns with the smirking grin held firm.

"What's with the stupid-ass grin?" questions the colonel. Wilhelm stares firm.

"Is that the question you wanted to ask?" Wilhelm asks in a tone of confirmation. "I'm not fully in control of my faculties yet. They're kind of doing their own thing right now." With a sigh, Colonel Telley lets go of Wilhelm's collar and takes a step back.

"What did they want to know and what do they look like?" asks Colonel Telley.

"We did not talk long, mostly the being asked questions about our home planet. How many of us there are -- as a collective race. They seem very inquisitive and desperate in wanting to know everything they can learn about us," he answers. "In my opinion of our first encounter shows them to be of no real threat to us."

"That's for me to decide," remarks the colonel. On this statement the colonel turns his back to Wilhelm and exits out the lab's door.

"Colonel," he calls. Telley stops midstep turning his view to Wilhelm. "I deem them no threat, which means I am still in charge of this goodwill mission and the alien communication device." This comment is said in a more authoritarian tone then Wilhelm has previously shown towards Colonel Telley.

"For now," replies Colonel Telley flatly. "I'm keeping my eye on you." Colonel Telley turns back to the door followed by his two thick branched arms shoving open the lab door banging it against the wall of the outer hall. After the medic gives Wilhelm one last quick going over he is escorted back to his quarters by the same stationed private. The door to his quarters shuts before he undresses and slips himself beneath the blanket-covered sheet lying over the twin mattress. Sleep evades him, forcing him to lie with his open eyes staring at the black ceiling tiles overlooking his quarters. The room is almost silent, except for the buzz of the orbiting station and the occasional passing muffled conversation on the outer side of his quarter's door.

Unaware to him is the fact he's being monitored at this very moment from a hidden camera behind a fake ventilation cover. The other end of the camera feed is fed to a scrawny communication tech monitoring the source camera along with one other located in the lab room housing the alien device. The room is little larger than a broom closet. No light to speak of, except from the twin monitors positioned on the makeshift desk connected to the nook's back wall. The door behind the chair occupied by the tech opens to reveal Colonel Telley towering in the light from the adjacent room.

"What has he done so far?" inquires the colonel.

"Just lying in bed staring at the ceiling, sir," replies the tech.

"Ok. Keep a sharp eye on him and tell me if he does anything out of the ordinary, private," commands the colonel.

"Yes, sir," answers the tech in a strict military tone.

"This is top secret. Don't speak a word to anyone or you'll be busted down to the waste-recycling sector, understood?" threatens the colonel. The tech simply answers with a double nod. Colonel Telley knows there's no way in hell anyone wants to be posted there. He went down there once for a build-up problem and he's never fully regained his sense of smell.

3.

The next day, after Wilhelm has crawled out of bed dressed in a new blue jumpsuit he returns to the machine room. The same lab tech from yesterday is already there retooling a few loose connections on the device.

"Are we ready to wire in?" Wilhelm inquires. The tech looks Wilhelm over from top to bottom. Rising up from behind the side of the machine the tech spends a moment pressing buttons and flipping switches until the monitoring console is ablaze with color. The tech turns his head and nods in assurance. Wilhelm moves into the proper position for the metal slab's restraints. Once he is strapped and secured the tech flips the appropriate switch activating the device, the restrained body spasms as his spiritual essence leaves his body once more. In a blink of time his spirit travels back to the gaseous planet for hours. The lab tech continues monitoring making sure everything remains stable and above the neutral line. The difference this time is when Wilhelm returns to his body there's no agonizing scream or violent spasm. He simply lifts his head from off his drool-covered chest. The side effects on this return are merely the slurring of speech, inability to maintain mobility, and loss of muscle control. On the whole nothing as severe as before, all side effects fade out around thirty minutes from his physical awareness. To be sure a medical team is ordered to examine him thoroughly as an added precaution.

From his monitoring room, Colonel Telley watches every second for any indication of looming danger to the station or mankind. He does not trust these alien lifeforms and his distrust of Wilhelm is ever increasing. *The jerks on Earth have no idea of the dangers they are welcoming down upon us. They only care for their own political careers and self aspirations to having their names entered into the history books. However, I fully realize the gravity of the situation and when the whole mess goes tits up. I'll be there ready to kick invader ass,* rants Colonel Telley's inner voice. His eyes stay fixed to the monitor. Closely studying Wilhelm's every movement. "What are you hiding from me?" he pounders in a whispered mumble.

Back in the lab, Wilhelm attempts to rise to his feet with aided assistance by the lab tech. "What did you talk about if you don't mind me asking?" probes the tech.

"There is work to do," remarks Wilhelm. "They have requested to speak with the leaders of the most powerful countries on Earth. We need to contact Earth and begin construction on other sets of devices to support multi-personnel transfer. Your job is to construct a wireless network hub between these devices and the network on this station."

"How am I going to do that?" replies the tech. His face is frozen in shock by this nearly impossible task just handed to him.

"They're going to send the specifications needed the same way they sent the ones for this device. You'll take what you need and redirect it to the appropriate facilities back on Earth," explains Wilhelm. He exits through the lab's door to step into the hallway and turns to his personal escort on his left. "I'm hungry. Where's the mess hall on this floating tomb?" The private directs him down the hall to their left towards a small crowd of people waiting for the elevator.

A few weeks have passed since the last communication with the alien lifeforms and work has proceeded exceptionally well. All of the powerful countries of the world are attending: United States, England, Russia, even China, to name a few. The whole world sits in unbridled excitement for Earth's first and fast-approaching galactic conference. Wilhelm is in communication with several department heads overseeing the construction of differing devices located across the surface of the planet.

"Are you all linked with the master device on the orbiting station?" he asks the various faces on the large monitor positioned in front of him. They all confirm they are linked, though they cannot reconnect. With this news, Wilhelm thunders down along the vacant corridors until he reaches his destination. Bursting through the lab door his sight sets on the tech diligently working away on a rat's nest of multi-colored cables and wires.

"Is there a problem?" questions Wilhelm rhetorically. The tech steps back from the wired nest filling the closet-sized compartment. He turns his attention to Wilhelm on setting his tool down besides the opening of the pile of wires.

"Well," he pauses momentarily as he hunts for the right collection of words. "Somewhere there is a short. It's an easy enough fix once I find the problem. As you can tell –" He pauses momentarily to hold up in his two hands the great mess of wires and cables. "That's easier said than done."

"We only have a couple of days before the conference. We don't need to short out in the middle of it. Get it fixed as soon as you can and let me know the moment it's finished?" orders Wilhelm. He turns towards the door.

"Sure thing," responds the tech as he dives back into the closet of wires. Wilhelm steps out of the lab and into the hall to come face to face with a different private who's standing next to Wilhelm's familiar escort.

"Excuse me sir. Colonel Telley requests you to come with me to his office for a meeting," greets the slightly older private.

"Tell Colonel Telley that with the conference only days away I don't have the time to meet with him. Ok private?" he replies. Shifting his feet to his right he begins to advance away from the private.

"I'm sorry, but it wasn't a question, sir," remarks the private in a stern voice. With a resigning shrug Wilhelm steps back to the two military men. The privates escort him along the hall to the left heading to the far end where Colonel Telley's office is located. On reaching the door the privates wait outside with Wilhelm stepping into the office. The station's most important civilian occupant shuts the door behind him after trudging in. Telley sits behind the same oak desk from their first meeting now covered by papers and photographs of various issues involving his multitude of duties aboard this station.

"What, may I ask is so important you had to speak to me now?" demands Wilhelm. Colonel Telley lifts his head up from his desk along with setting down the thick stack of papers held in his hand.

"How much sleep have you had since your first meeting?" asks the colonel calmly.

"Not sure. Not as much as I should be getting, I'd say. I do have a lot on my plate right now," replies Wilhelm calmly. Colonel Telley leans back in his chair stretching his arms up and back as he lets out a loud yawn. Wilhelm just stands in the middle of the room looking to him in an almost puzzled expression.

"Do you think the aliens sleep?" asks Telley, while lowering his arms back to his side to rest them on the surface of his messy oak desk.

"Don't know. They are formless entity beings. My general opinion would have to be that of no," he guesses in the best way he knows how. Wilhelm begins to feel anxious about these bizarre questions Colonel Telley is posing. "I'm sorry, where is this line of questioning heading?"

"None, really," remarks Telley. This time wasting conversation is starting to annoy Wilhelm. He takes a deep breath and exhales one solemn release to give him time to calm his rising outrage.

"If there is no point to this talk then I'm sorry, sir. I've got more important things to do," he snaps. He starts for the office door.

"Hold it right there," orders the colonel. Wilhelm stops and turns back to face Telley. "When I said none, I wasn't answering your question. I was answering my question. You haven't logged, but twenty-five hours of sleep in almost five weeks. Now, I find it very odd you are able to still work as diligently as you are. Or for that matter how you are even still able to stand on your two feet without falling face first to the floor."

"What makes you so sure of your number, colonel?" he asks.

"I have the lab and your quarters under twenty-four hour surveillance," he replies with a sly grin. "What did they do to you? I haven't quite figured it out myself, but it will only be a matter of time."

"You are paranoid. I can't believe you'd go so far as to have my quarters bugged. You have no authority to order such a command. I can sympathize with you becoming outraged over being treated like a second-class citizen involving anything taking place on your station. This does not, however, give you the right to bug anything having to do with my division on this station," Wilhelm states with ample attitude. Turning out the door he charges back down the hall with the door slamming shut in his wake. Advancing down the sterilized white corridors Wilhelm stops next to a door with a gold nameplate, which reads *Communication Room*. Entering inside he takes a seat on a black and red stationary swivel chair in front of a global communication unit. Placing the system's headset over his ears he starts turning the knobs to fix onto an exact frequency. A moment later he rests the dials on the desired frequency. "Goodwill Expedition to Galactic High Command, Earth Station."

"Galactic High Command, Earth Station to Goodwill Expedition we read you," returns a voice over the communication's headset.

"I need to speak to General Winslow, urgently," he replies.

"What's this in regards to?" asks the voice.

"It's in regards to Colonel Telley's interference with the expedition," he answers.

"Just a moment," returns the voice over the headset. He waits less than a minute before the General's voice speaks into his headset. With the upcoming conference the General stands at a seconds notice from the coms unit if any problems should arise. Colonel Telley has become the number one perpetrator for this action.

"What has he done now?" greets the general in a voice of great announce.

4.

Later that day, Wilhelm is once again in the communications room speaking with his various contacts on Earth about the work still needing to be completed before the conference being held in a few short days. He signs off at the precise moment Colonel Telley bursts in from the hallway running outside of the communications door. He strides across the room to Wilhelm, who's rising from the comfort of the stationary chair. Colonel Telley with three shoves of full-force positions Wilhelm against the room's far wall. He tries to deflect Telley's attack, but he is no match for Telley. His slams against the unforgiving wall with a loud shot of pain firing up his back.

"What's wrong with you?" poses Wilhelm, while trying to stabilize his footing.

"I finished speaking with General Winslow. He told me you communicated to him that I'm endangering the expedition's mission," he bellows.

"Yeah I did, your constant interference is costing us needed hours for unneeded delays," he responses flatly.

"What's the real reason for this massive meeting of the world's top leaders?" he demands. "Are they planning an invasion or are they going to try and kill them all," the colonel theorizes through a tone filled with frustration.

"You are fully paranoid, colonel. You've well established that fact," he remarks with the last half containing an air of sympathy.

"What's that supposed to mean, pissant," snaps Telley.

"I've read your file, Colonel," he discloses without hesitation. "General Winslow thought it a good idea after our last disagreement." Wilhelm speaks with Telley moving closer. In all honest truth he's closer than Wilhelm would like him to be.

"And what would a little pissant civilian now about my experiences?" counters Colonel Telley with a sharp tongue. He doesn't wait for an answer before he back tracks to his previous inquiry. "I want to know everything you've learned about them."

"Firstly, that's not going to happen. I would like to reiterate again. What I've tried to explain to you on many different occasions. You're not in charge here, colonel. I don't answer to you. This is my assignment. I've been entrusted with this honor and I wish you'd accept it," reemphasizes Wilhelm in the most politely calm voice he can muster at the moment.

"You haven't been entrusted with anything. The only reason you're heading this farce of an expedition is because you had your head crammed up frequencies you had no business meddling with in the first place. Yes. I've read your crappy excuse of a file too," barks the colonel. The lower part of the colonel's right arm pins Wilhelm's neck against the firm wall. The hold begins cutting off the airway causing Wilhelm to try desperately to push off Telley's attack with both hands applying force away from his neck. This action has little effect against Colonel Telley's enraged strength as the pressure mounts. Wilhelm's head starts to throb from the lack of needed oxygen. His eyesight has become speckled with tiny dots of burning light. When it would seem his time has come the door opens to reveal a communications officer stepping into the room. On seeing the current situation, he springs into action pulling Colonel Telley off of Wilhelm. The officer has to deal with only a small amount of resistance from the seasoned colonel. Wilhelm collapses to the floor in a frantic spasm trying to fill his lungs. Wilhelm greedily inhales air causing his throat to burn along his already inflamed throat; all while hording the oxygen down into his sacks of tissue.

"What's going on here?" questions the officer. Neither man gives him an adequate answer. "I'm afraid I'm going to have to call the MP's."

"Good captain. Lock this man in his quarters until we figure out what to do with him," directs the equally winded colonel. He stands over the shriveling civilian with a sanctimonious grin.

"I mean both of you, colonel. Until there is proper time for the military council to review the surveillance tape," corrects the captain with further clarification. Colonel Telley's grin quickly vanishes beneath his war-ravaged leather skin.

"You do that, captain," remarks the colonel in anger. "Before the council convenes. I'll have the issue taken care of long before they ever review the facts." With that said Colonel Telley storms through the room's door to disappear into the white hall behind. The captain turns his attention on Wilhelm and helps him to his feet.

"Your throat is badly bruised. Let's get you checked out in the Infirmary," suggests the captain. On his suggestion the two men exit and move along the hall to the Infirmary. Wilhelm's left arm is wrapped behind the captain's neck to help him walk.

After an hour on pure oxygen Wilhelm receives a call from General Winslow on a remote com's unit located within the Infirmary. Removing the oxygen mask he speaks with the general, although his voice is still heavily hoarse from the assault.

"How are you boy?" asks the general with a whisper of concern.

"Fine general," he affirms. "I simply have a renewed love for breathing, that's all."

"Good to hear you've still got your sense of humor. Now I, myself, have reviewed the surveillance footage and it's quite clear Colonel Telley initiated the confrontation. From what you have already reported I don't think it's hard to arrive at the collective decision to remove him from his post and to undergo a psychiatric evaluation," he remarks. "I will send his replacement immediately. He should arrive within ten hours."

"General with all due respect, I don't think that will be necessary or advisable," he remarks respectfully. "With two days left before the conference. Changing leadership staff will only give greater upheaval to the station's chain of command and efficiency. Colonel Telley's skeptical worries have escalated into this aggressive outburst over his deep-seeded concerns brought on by his delusion to the alien's supposed secretive purposes. I think it advisable for the station and for Colonel Telley's own mental health to allow him, before the conference, to meet with the beings." Wilhelm waits for what seems to be several minutes as the general mulls over Wilhelm's imaginative solution.

"Your suggestion is bold and risky. However, your explanation sounds like the best course of action to take for at least Colonel Telley's sake. When do you think you'll be ready?" asks the general.

"Definitely no sooner than twenty-four hours, providing Colonel Telley does not interfere any further," he answers.

"If he does he's going to be court-marshaled to the highest extent possible. Alright, I'll talk to him about the situation," says the general.

"General! I would just like to ask when you do talk with him. Don't mention it's my suggestion. If he knows it is my idea he will most likely refuse. He's under the impression I'm in cahoots with the alien's plans."

"I won't tell him. Now, if you're feeling up to it would you please get back to work," he inquires.

"Right away, General Winslow, over and out," responses Wilhelm. He stands up from off the chair and walks with a slowness in his step down the hall heading back to the lab to check-in on the wiring mess.

5.

Ten hours to conference, Wilhelm stands with the lab tech warming up the machine in wait for Colonel Telley's arrival. Ten minutes of further waiting passes before Colonel Telley strolls through the lab door with an overbearing grin set from ear to ear.

"What are we waiting for gentlemen?" he asks rhetorically with his smug face gleaming. The lab tech directs him to the restraint slab and begins strapping him in. "Does it burn you to have me here? General Winslow informed me how furious you objected when he told you he wished for me to make sure everything checks out clean. Entrusted with this assignment? Huh! In the end it falls back to me." The tech straps Wilhelm into the second restraint slab to the left of the colonel.

"Ready, sirs?" asks the tech to both men. Wilhelm is first to answer with a nod.

"Yes, now let's get on with it," snaps the colonel.

"Sir, the first time can be very violent," explains the tech.

"If this pissant can take it, so can I. Let's get on with it already," he orders.

"Telley, there is something I want you to know," says Wilhelm allowing a pause to drift in. "I suggested to the general for you to take this trip." His words flow into Colonel Telley's ears in a whisper mere seconds before the tech flips the activation switch. Telley's face turns from smug to fear-stricken the second before their bodies begin to spasm violently.

Colonel Telley floats alone in the same gaseous planet's foggy vapor where Wilhelm has done so many times before. He's awestruck by the blue glow he's emitting. Lifting his hand halfway to his face he finds he can see right through. It's from here he notices through the translucent flesh of his hand an elongated figure approaching him amongst the foggy mist. The colonel looks to his left and right, but Wilhelm is nowhere to be found. The being moves ever closer filling him with a helpless feeling of fright by this approaching figure. Looking back over his shoulder he searches for any other glowing forms approaching who might be Wilhelm. All he finds is a long string of light he reasons leads back to his material form. It's his energy trail keeping the link between his now separated parts that form his singular being. At last, in the distant vapor behind him he sees a faint glow of an approaching entity from behind. Colonel Telley turns back to see the featureless silhouette standing, waiting for his attention.

"My names Colonel William H. Telley, I'm commander aboard the space station O'Leary," he says with nervous apprehension. The being stands motionless and unspoken. The entity of Wilhelm halts to his left, "What's wrong with it? It just stands there doing nothing. How can it talk, hear, or even see me if it has no face?" Telley turns his view to his companion. "Are you going to answer me –" His voice vanishes mid-sentence on seeing the shocking revelation of the too long masked truth standing beside him.

"Your quite anxious colonel," comments the green glowing entity to the colonel's left with the use of telepathy. "Just in case you were wondering my name is Glandda. I'm the spirit that has been residing within Wilhelm Gilroy's material form for the last few weeks."

"So, I was right!" he replies through thought.

"Yes, well, only in general terms. The fine details are slightly askew. What we are going to implement in a few short hours is the peaceful takeover of every form in your leadership. With their forms as our vessels we shall have ample access to activate your planet's nuclear reserves and begin cultivating your world for our distant arrival within the coming months," Glandda explains. "In fact, you will be changing from your previous stance on the matter to one where you will fully support and help aid us to carry out this agenda."

"The hell I will! I'm going to put an end to this the moment I get back," refutes Colonel Telley with all the anger he can conjure.

"Yes. You are partially right about that too," remarks Glandda. "Let's just say, to your fellow humans you will be helping us. You see, we are the ones in control of these devices. You can't leave unless we allow it. Your station is very important to our objectives. To this fact I'm afraid we're going to have to, oh what's your word, oh yes, terminate your existence."

The lanky being standing in front of them pulls a spherical device located in its right hand. One of its elongated fingers presses a button. The tip of the device builds with an ever growing green ball of electrical light. On reaching its max capacity the electrical ball releases and speeds to connect with Colonel Telley. When it hits his chest he screams in absolute agony as his glowing entity is forcefully torn from its energy trail separating his one form from his material form. His fading entity fizzles until he evaporates into the foggy vapor leaving an open energy trail to his material self. The being, which held the spherical device, moves to the open end of the energy trail turning its back to the light blue trail. The alien entity attaches itself in what was once Colonel Telley.

Meanwhile in the lab, the tech unhooks the colonel from the metal slab restraint with assistance from the medical team preemptively on call in the lab. His vitals have flatlined just like Wilhelm's had on his first trip. The medics are working on the colonel when Wilhelm rejoins his body.

"Leave him be. His entity has to rejoin with his body," he states to the medical team. The lab tech unhooks Wilhelm and after twenty minutes the colonel breathes new life into his body.

"Are you alright, sir?" asks the tech. He's able to answer with only a weak nod of his head. The medical team wheels him to the Infirmary for some monitored rest. After four hours. Colonel Telley returns to his duties. Sitting at his desk he works diligently as his personal assistant enters the colonel's office.

"Colonel Telley? General Winslow is on the com for you," he reports. Spinning in place he steps back out the door. The colonel sets down his pen and flicks on the remote communication system to the right of his desk.

"General Winslow -- Colonel Telley here, sir," he says into the system.

"How are you feeling old boy?" asks the general.

"Perfect, sir," he replies.

"Glad to hear you in such good spirits. I was afraid you were nearing your last mental leg of your career. Anyway down to business. With only a few remaining hours what's your opinion? Is the conference a go or rather are they of good intentions?" asks the old voice.

"Everything is on the up and up, General," answers Colonel Telley. "Let's make history."

"Glad to hear it. Glad to hear it. I can't wait for our fishing trip next month, I'll see you then," finishes the general.

"Can't wait, sir," returns Colonel Telley. He switches off the unit. Turning his attention to his left he looks at Wilhelm who's sitting on a black stationary chair in the far corner of the office. "It's all set, the time has come to sit back and enjoy the ride." Telley leans back putting his hands behind the back of his head. Wilhelm rises from out of the chair and advances to the office door. On opening it he turns back toward the new entity housed in Colonel Telley's body. The two men exchange sinful grins followed with Wilhelm leaving the room on his way to the lab to execute the most covert global takeover in the history of the galaxy.

Unwanted Escort

At a lit full-service gas station its two attending employees are seconds away from shutting down for the day. The sun has nearly set behind the tree-covered hills spanning the distant horizon. The last remains of the day splash across its multi-colored sky blanketing the surrounding woods neighboring the station. One of the two men turn off the large plastic street sign immediately followed by a puttering wood-paneled station wagon creeping in and stopping at one of the eight pumps. The older of the two men steps out from the station's metal building positioned to the middle of the concrete island between two pumps.

"Sorry we're closed for the night," he states to the man stepping out the front passenger door.

"Oh please, we've used up all the leftover fumes?" the man pleads, as he stands behind the open door.

"Hold on," replies the old man. He steps back inside the metal building before stretching his top half back out through the crack in the doorway. "Since we haven't turned off the pumps, go ahead. Make it quick we'd like to head home."

"Sure, of course," the man returns as he hurries to the pump to pour in twenty bucks worth. His wife, who's sitting in the driver's seat hands the old man a twenty along with two extra ten dollar bills. One ten for each attendant for their obliging nature to a car of strangers. After a pleasant and short exchange of farewells the car advances to the end of the gravel drive. The wagon pulls out onto the now darkening river of asphalt forming Route One.

Within the wagon the young couple drives along the strip of asphalt without a care in the world. In the back section behind the middle bench seat of the wagon is the makeshift sleeping quarters for their two little girls. Audrey and Bridget, who are both fast asleep beneath a red flannel blanket. Dreaming of castles, ponies, and white knights along with all the other things little girls surely dream about with their father periodically checking on them from time to time by looking over the passenger seat. A grin forms as he thinks how cute they look when they are fast asleep in the world of their own undisturbed happiness. He repositions himself until his cheeks are securely planted on the base of the seat. Looking out at the unfolding terrain ahead that rolls from out of the advancing darkness and into the wagon's bright headlights. Again he shifts his focus, but this time it is centered on his life-saving angel behind the wheel.

"How are you doing?" he asks in a sincere tone with his left hand massaging the back of her neck.

"I'm fine. Though I'm getting a little drowsy I could really use a Mocha Latte," she answers knowing her suggestion won't be fulfilled anytime soon.

"I know what'cha mean," he replies. Even though he hates any kind of coffee product he can still relate to her need for a jolt of caffeine.

"So what did you think of Scott?" she asks him in a trying attempt to keep her mind awake.

"Scott who?" he questions back.

"You know, Scott, my sister's new husband. They just got married four hours ago and that's why we're driving home right this instance. That Scott!" she taunts. Her voice fills with a momentary annoyance towards him for doing his own level best to zone off. She doesn't blame him; they've been up since four-thirty this morning. What annoys her most is he's starting what she positively cannot. Those situations are what really annoy her. She snaps out of her inner rant on realizing he's answering.

"He seems nice. I only spoke to him for about ten minutes. It's not nearly long enough to have a life-long bond or even a full psychological evaluation," he answers. "I look at it this way. If he wants to take your psychotic sister away from us let him."

"I'm just worried, she hasn't had the best luck in picking men with good character," she comments.

"That's certainly true. Wait, what about the cocaine-addicted biker ex-gang member. You can't find anyone with more character then him," he teases accompanied by his signature smirking grin. The two of them share a chuckle at remembering that first meeting.

"Yeah, definitely was a nightmare," she says. A pair of headlights near them forces her to click off her high beams, more out of habit then courtesy. The car quickly passes by. The car's lights pass over the back half of the station wagon; this causes her to think she spotted something from the corner of her eye in the center of the rearview mirror. With her eyes widening and her chuckle abruptly cut short her husband can see the change in expression and knows something has put her off.

"Honey, what's the matter?" he questions with genuine concern. Turning his head to look out the back window he sees nothing, only the night's consuming darkness.

"I swear, I just saw that car's headlights bounce off of something directly behind us," she explains along with her thumb pointing over her right shoulder to the back window.

"You mean reflected off the window?" he asks in an attempt to understand what she's implying.

"Yes reflected. No. Not off OUR back window," she doubles down. He turns back to the rear window and this time studiously looks out into the darkness filling the window.

"I still don't see anything, hon'," he replies in a sympathetic, but disbelieving tone.

"Fine. Be a jerk and don't believe me I could care less. I saw what I saw and that's that," she responds in an aggravated tone.

"I didn't say I don't believe you. All I know is I don't see anything behind us," he states in a defensive tone. The wagon on making the next sharp right reveals two white lights burning through the darkness heading their way.

"Ok. Keep your eyes out the back and when the light passes you'll see what I'm talking about," she explains. With a nod in agreement her husband positions himself to get a better look out the back. With every second that passes the duel lights of the approaching vehicle grow larger and closer. The air surrounding the young couple is filling with a tightening weight of anxiety. Each passing second causes her to grow more anxious in the desperate hope to bring validation to her own eyes and mind. The lights are less than ten feet from passing the front of the wagon.

What transpires next happens in only a matter of seconds, but it feels like minutes for the young couple. She watches as the headlights tiptoe across the wagon's hood. The lights jump onto the driver's wood-paneled door to proceed to race along the length of the wagon's rectangular form to then jump off of the wagon's red plastic brake light. It is in this moment, her heart along with her breathing stops in agonizing wait for the terrorizing phantom reflection to reveal itself from the back window. It is here the light ricochets momentarily off of a reflective surface positioned directly behind them. Upon seeing her terror justified she painfully exhales as her heart rises into the middle of her throat.

"Did you see that? Oh please, tell me you saw what I saw?" she desperately says. Her husband doesn't respond not even one word escapes from out of his frozen expression. Turning back onto his seat he stares vacantly ahead. "Well?"

"Yeah, I saw it. What is it?" he asks not expecting an answer. Then as if a light bulb goes off above his head. He opens the glove compartment and rummages around in the disastrous mess lying within.

"What are you doing?" she asks with a tone almost questioning his sanity. This line of thought in itself is humorous, being she posed the same question to herself mere seconds ago.

"I'm going to lean back there and shine this flashlight out the window and see what's there," he explains in a hurried speech.

"Good idea, Babe," she replies. Turning back to face the window he extends himself as far back as he can. So far, in fact, his right arm needs to hold his top half up above his sleeping angels. With the emergency flashlight in his left hand he extends his arm to get as close to the window without having to jump back there. Once he's steady as her driving will allow him to be. He switches on the flashlight pointing it dead center out the window. At first he can't make anything out because of the natural reflection of the wagon's own glass. But, finally, he comes face to face with what's trailing along behind them. He pans the light to the right and looks into the face of a beard-covered middle-aged man behind a black steering wheel. He can't make out the man's exact features, because he instantly covers his face with his left hand, palm facing the light. In his shock, he jumps back hitting the back of his head against the wagon's ceiling light.

"What is it? What did you see?" she asks in worry.

"A man," he replies in a whisper of shock.

"A . . . what?" she yells as the car slightly rocks back and forth down the road, due to her sudden increase in anxiety. "What should I do, pull over?" She removes her foot from off the gas pedal and shifts to the brake.

"No!" he yells in hurried prevention causing her to replace her foot on the gas pedal with a momentary boost to the car's acceleration. " Don't do that. If you do, one of two things will happen. First, it could be exactly what he wants and is waiting for you to do. Second, if you slam on the brakes at this rate of speed mixed with how close he is, well, you can figure out the rest."

"Fine," she replies. Pushing her foot down the vehicle increases its already high rate of speed. "Is he still behind us?" her eyes continuously dart from the road ahead to the black-filled rearview mirror.

"Yes," he answers after checking.

"I got it," she blurts out in a tone of self-realization. "If he wants to follow us, he can. He can follow us straight to the Trooper's station,"

"That could work," he adds. Turning back to the front he looks out the windshield at the rolling terrain coming from out of the darkness positioned ahead of their bright headlights.

"The turn is to the right in less than one hundred feet," he answers as he scoots slightly forward, as if, he can see further down the road this way. They continue at the speed of seventy-five miles an hour. It's only a few seconds before the once grassy corner of the road opens onto an intersecting road to the right. "There!" He directs with his right index finger pointing the way. His wife turns the wheel as sharp as the wagon will allow. The tires squeal as the wagon tries desperately to make the ninety degree turn. The two of them hold tight as they are pulled with tremendous force to their left. From the back of the wagon he can hear two moans of pinned pressure as the once sleeping princesses have been tossed to the far left from the force of the turn. Just when the wagon appears it may not make the turn its back end finally evens out with the intersecting street. Her eyes are thrown to her rearview mirror once the vehicle is stable. She watches as the once stalking truck's silhouette continues straight on Route One and does not turn to follow. Her tension-filled heart slowly lowers back into her chest at viewing this development. A slight chuckle escapes her puckered lips as a thought forms in her mind.

"What if he wasn't following us?" she thinks out loud. Her husband stops to ponder this for a moment. By this time the two sleepy-headed girls are up from the rude awakening they received.

"What was that?" asks Audrey in a sleepy voice. Neither parent acknowledges her probing question. "Hello?"

"Honey just go back to sleep," he orders. With a sunken face she lowers back down behind the unfolded middle bench seat. She's momentarily followed by her younger sister. For the rest of the ride home the once happy young couple sits wide awake not speaking a word. They follow the ever unfolding terrain, which hides in the never-ending dark of this Maine road.

Four miles away from where the terrifying nightmare ended an elderly man locks the glass door of his ma & pa auto parts store signaling the end of a reasonable day of business. He scoots away from the door over to the farthest window to his right to flick off the power switch for the store's open sign. Pulling down on the switch the blue and yellow neon sign turns off. He hears someone laying ruthlessly on a loud truck horn. The old geezer squints out the sign's window to see an old GMC truck painted flat black rolling across the store's gravel drive. The strangest thing he thinks to himself is the truck's lights are off. A light slowly turns on above his head like a slow warming fluorescent tube. Scooting back over to the door and with a couple clicks he unlocks it from its metal frame. Opening the door he greets the middle-aged bearded man exiting his truck to enter the auto parts store.

"Back again, Roger?" comments the old man as he locks the door behind the unexpected arrival.

"Yeah, the damn wiring system shorted out, again. I had to drive danger close behind an old station wagon for most of the run down here," he explains. He follows the old man to the store's counter.

"I told you not to buy the cheap Chinese wiring system," states the old man.

"Yeah, yeah, can I hitch a ride and leave my truck here until the morning?" asks Roger.

"Sure, just give me a minute to tally up," replies the old man. "Did you know those who you were following?"

"No," Roger answers. "They shined a damn light out the back window blinding me and nearly sending me off the road. Then they sped up to seventy-five miles an hour. They took the turn onto Edgewater off Route One at fifty-five miles an hour. Damn lucky the fools didn't roll the thing."

"Drivers today, phooey. The laws of the road go right out the window with most of 'em," he comments, while he starts to calculate what is held in the cash box.

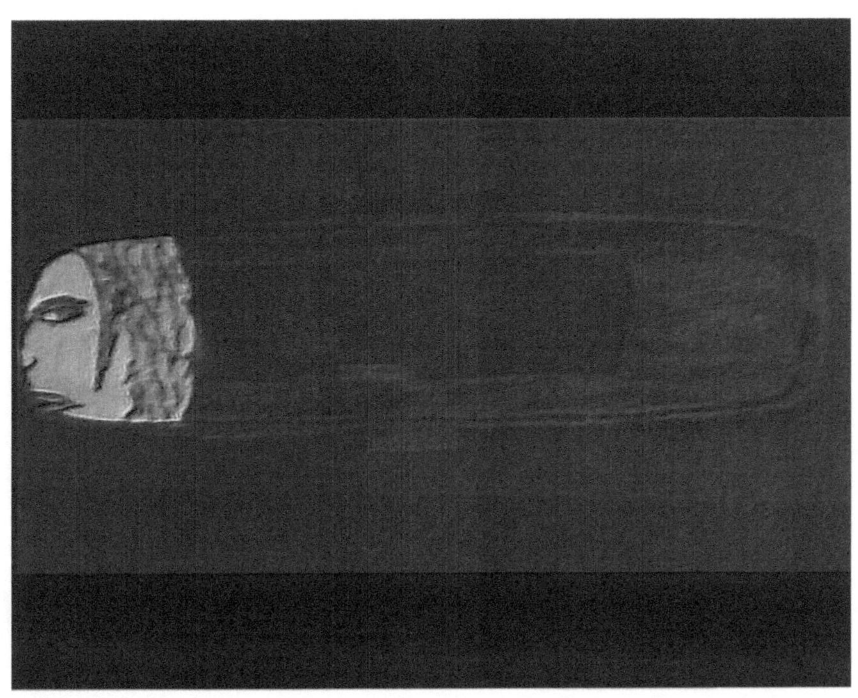

Heart-Broke Martyr

Deep within our love hides.
    Our souls uncontrollably entwined.
As our bodies collide, we savor the ride.
So we formed the mold.
A marriage that's bright and bold.
To have and to hold, for all we could afford.
In a life filled with frenzy.
We came to fancy.
A life of plenty, but without a family.
A childless mother.
With emotions smothered.
She blames the father, for her thought of 'why bother'.
My precious queen.
My helpless being.
Why do I have the feeling, our love's fleeting?
It's her sadness.
That brought my madness.
Taking him upon the mattress, before me with a heart of malice.
A satisfying bloodlust splatter.
Crime of a heart-broken martyr.
Oh god! How I have faltered, but it's too late to alter.
My blood-soaked hands.
Hang above the sinful damned.
Showing off their command, to prove I'm no lesser a man.

The Captain's Untimely Promotion

1. "Lieutenant Harvey Nicholas?" asks a young boy in pristine tidiness. The kind of cleanliness expected from a member of Her Majesty's Royal Navy when addressing a superior naval officer.

"Yes, I'm Lieutenant Nicholas," he answers back. On this response, the young lad hands a wax-sealed letter to the lieutenant. He takes the letter from the boy with his right hand and immediately places it into his lower outer pocket of his blue naval woolen coat. "Thank you, my lad." Before the boy parts from Nicholas's sight he's given a few shillings in reward of his errand. "I know how poorly you're paid to lick you commander's boot heels. Let's keep this between you and me, ok?" With an enormous grin he nods with enthusiasm immediately followed by the boy running off out of sight. *He's probably going to stop somewhere before his master notices he's missing and buy some sweets*, theorizes Nicholas.

"Who's the letter from?" asks the lieutenant's greasy looking friend, who's accompanying him to the local tavern.

"A letter from Admiral Jones, probably chastising me for the career ending nocturnal antics that occurred two evenings ago," suggests Nicholas with shameful humiliation hidden in his voice. He pulls the sealed letter from his coat pocket. Abruptly and without warning, he can hear the voice of his first captain he ever served under. *Damn it Harvey, that's no way for a respectable officer of the Royal Navy to present himself.* He used to spout this short lecture whenever Nicholas would do something foolish or dumb. Nicholas also reflects on the fact he'd never worked harder then when he was under his command. Though he tried to save his captain on that fateful day he was simply a few seconds too late. He watched as his mentor was crushed under the weight of the Spaniard's main mast as it landed on top of him. The only other captain to have ever gained his total respect was Captain Aubrey. He is jolted back from his thoughts by his comrade's firm tap on the shoulder.

"That's not Admiral Jones's wax seal," observantly comments the lieutenant's friend. He speaks in a tone not to insult, but to educate his companion. Nicholas pulls the letter from out his pocket to look longer at the seal located on the back of the letter. His face brightens into a smile on recognizing the seal. The lieutenant notices the change in his companion's expression. "What is it?" Nicholas breaks the seal of the letter with a flick of his finger and reads the message scribbled within the folded paper. "What does it say?"

"It's from Admiral Aubrey," he replies. "He has taken over command of this port from Admiral Jones. He's been reassigned to a different port closer to Spain. Admiral Aubrey requests my company this evening to discuss my naval future in Her Majesty's fleet."

"Well, I guess that could be good news," remarks the lieutenant with slight curiosity as to why Nicholas is so pleased with such a vague letter.

"It most certainly is my good man. It's great news!" he returns in a heighten tone.

"I'm sorry, I still don't get what's so great about the letter," he confesses. Nicholas has now quickened his pace to the tavern, which had been their original destination before the news of the letter arrived. The tavern has been Lieutenant Nicholas' port of call for the past few months as he has anxiously awaited his next naval assignment. However, due to his attitude and reputation amongst the port's captaincy he has been finding it harder and harder to locate a willing commander who will take him onto their quarterdeck. He knows he only has himself to blame for this career leprosy.

"I've known Admiral Aubrey since he first became captain. He was the only one besides my first captain who pushed me to go beyond my best. They both helped mold me into becoming the most skilled man on a man-o-war second only to the ship's highest-level officer," Nicholas explains with enough detail to show the strong connection between them. "My career plague will soon be at an end." With that heightened note, the two companions step through the entrance to the tavern to cheer his newfound fortune.

Following an afternoon fueled by semi-controlled boozing, Nicholas staggers back to his room located across the street and up one flight of murderous steps. Falling onto his goose-feathered mattress he passes out before his head hits the pillow. This series of events obviously causes him to miss his appointment with his old mentor.

2.

Nicholas is woken by hard knocks coming from the other side of his door. Opening the door he finds two naval officers in full dress standing in the hall.

"Lieutenant Nicholas, your presence is requested by Admiral Aubrey immediately," relays the officer to Nicholas's left. The two officers look Nicholas in the eye as though they're waiting for his refusal. Sensing the tension they're aiming in his direction he gives a single nod.

"Let me gather my coat," Nicholas answers. He starts to close the door when the officer on the left puts his hand out blocking the door from shutting.

"We're under strict orders to not let you out of our sight," informs the officer. With this said he leaves the door ajar, while grabbing his coat. The three men move down the hall on their way to the port admiral's headquarters. On their arrival at the admiral's office the officers leave Nicholas to see the admiral on his own. Cautiously he enters the room knocking three times as it gradually opens. The room is dark due to the curtains being drawn. The only light is from two oil lamps positioned one to each side of the admiral's hand-carved oak desk. The admiral sits behind the desk on a matching oak chair. Nicholas can't make out his characteristic features due to the dim lighting his eyes are still trying to adjust. He closes the door and salutes him, which after a time is returned. Without having one word uttered Nicholas takes a seat on one of the two chairs directly in front of the menacing oak desk. Admiral Aubrey still says nothing for several minutes, while he puffs away at his wooden pipe. Nicholas is reminded upon seeing this picture of the admiral that the pipe is Aubrey's one and only true vice. He would rip ten seaman's heads clean off if he didn't have his morning pipe. After finishing his smoke and cleaning out the remaining bits he begins to speak to the fully un-nerved Nicholas.

"We may have known each other some years back and I can't help, but to feel slightly favorable towards you. However, that does not give you license to choose whether or not to see me. You are under my command and when by hell you are ordered to attend a gathering in order to discuss your -- let's say catastrophic military history and your ever growing uncertain future in Her Majesty's Royal Navy., You'd better damn well be prompt on the order!" finishes Aubrey with his face in an extreme shade of red. Admiral Aubrey tilts his head slightly up followed by a deep relaxing inhale and exhale. Without saying an-other word he leans forward into the light of the lamps looks the lieu-tenant square in the eyes with a solemn grin. Nicholas can now clearly see the admiral's physical scars from surviving both years at sea and military engagements.

His right eye, including its pupil, has lost its once beautiful sky blue coloring. It's been replaced with a white haze clouding his sight. He's seen many a man with this problem. In the heat of battle it is normally caused by a shower of splinters created by an unseen rogue cannon-ball landing nearby. The certainty he knows is with this kind of injury there's no way he can see anything on his right side without turning to look with his left eye.

"I see you've noticed my reason for desk-a-tood. It happened when we were assisting a merchant ship from Norway, which was under siege by three Spanish man-o-wars. The battle wasn't even the slightest bit equal," begins Admiral Aubrey. Nicholas knows Aubrey well enough to know when he's about to tell a tale of honorable glory. "That day the sea was in our favor. Not only was the wind to our backs, but we had the element of surprise for we were hidden under the cover of the rising sun. We came down on top of the first man-o-war without her even knowing we were there and took out her mainsail with one precise cannonball strike. It fell onto the foresail mast and created a dominoes effect causing all of the ship's masts to either buckle or to be in an unusable condition. In other words, the first Spaniard ship was out of the fight before the skirmish had even commenced. We turned our attention onto the next closest ship, though; naturally our element of surprise had been lost. The second ship had already turned about and was barring down upon us. I ordered the ship to pull to the starboard side of the Spaniard's vessel for a powerful broadside –" He's interrupted by a knock from the room's door forcing him to stop his heroic tale. "Enter!" The door opens with slight hesitation due to the admiral's tone. The admiral's personal aide enters the room from the other side of the door. He's a greenhorn looking piece of adolescent boy hiding in a slightly older man's body.

"Just to remind the admiral, sir, in ten minutes you have a meeting with the port captain, sir," the aide comments in a shallow voice. The admiral nods and with a wave of his hand the aide closes the door just as silent as a whisper.

"Sometimes I wonder who's in charge the admiral or his aide?" asks Admiral Aubrey in a rhetorical tone. "I was hoping to have a longer engagement of time to discuss these matters in length with you. But -- I have other pressing matters I have to attend to shortly. My predecessor saved this disciplinary report from three nights previous involving two captains' wives and one goat," Admiral Aubrey gives a slight pause to look at Nicholas as he once more reviews the report. "My predecessor strongly suggests, considering your miserable military history along with your many problems with authority. Imprisonment into a Spaniard-filled prison or marooned on a quarantined island he felt was well deserved. Upon looking at your record I couldn't agree more with his recommendations. According to naval law these sentences are more than fitting punishments, but he doesn't know your personal hardships like I do." He looks firmly at Nicholas to mentally emphasis this is his absolute last chance. "I'm sure it's been extremely hard to see the last three corps of young officers pass you in rank. I feel that best explains your rowdy way of living for these last several years." At the same time, as he makes this statement he holds up the report with his left hand. "On this reason alone is why I've spoken to my last lieutenant who has taken command of the Majesty's Pride. He's agreed to take you on for the next few months to serve as his first lieutenant -- you are to be second only to him. If you can make it through this tour without causing any more problems we'll talk about you getting you own captaincy."

"Thank you, Admiral Aubrey, sir," farewells Nicholas, while rising from his chair. He salutes the admiral and crosses the room to stop beside the door. His right hand grips the doorknob and spins his torso to look over his shoulder to his old mentor. "Admiral Aubrey, sir?" The admiral looks up from the papers covering his desk.

"Yes, Nicholas?" replies the admiral. He looks to the lieutenant with a look asking why he's still here.

"I was just wondering what was the outcome of the skirmish besides your physical scars?" he asks. Aubrey's face forms a wide grin in response to reliving his last naval battle.

"In the end, we sank the second ship after a few volleys of cannon fire. The third Spaniard ship tucked tail and ran on a fast blowing wind. They were only able to escape, due to the previous clash causing us to receive a critical hit just above our waterline," he summarizes.

"So, when did you get that?" he asks as he points his index and middle finger of his left hand just under his own right eye. Upon hearing this question the admiral recalls the painful answer. His grin quickly recedes beneath his scrawny lips.

"The third ran, but before we drifted too far apart she shot one last cannon. The ball collided with the wood below where I was standing. The last thing I remember seeing from my right eye was a cloud of splintered wood flying toward me," he explains trailed by his view returning back to his stack of papers. On this farewell Nicholas opens the door and exits from the office accompanied closely by his departure from the admiral's headquarters. In having every intention to keep within the predetermined arrangement, which will relaunch his appalling career, he returns to his room at the port's barracks to pack his few belongings in preparation for his deployment off this island.

Around eight that night, Nicholas has had to already turn down four offers of drink from his landlocked brethren with prize money burning holes in their pockets. Refusing the bottles was a lot less difficult then he figured it would be. What helps the most to stay away from his prize-filled mates is the excitement of once again climbing aboard a ship. It's been almost two and a half months since he last felt the cooling sea breeze cutting passed his cheeks. The desire for the open sea has always been his greatest thrill and this being his last chance for command he has no plans to deviate from the admiral's conditions. He sleeps very little his growing need to board his new home is making him anxious. Even now she drifts out in the harbor on a two day furlough, due to needed repairs. *If this arrangement is all a dream then I don't want to wake up.* Finally around two he falls into sleep dreaming of his new captain and his subsequent first mate duties.

The next day at the break of dawn he awakens and is out the door with his few petty belongings. He advances to the docks to speak with the dock master to negotiate the use of one of the pier's rowboats. A few minutes more, he is rowed out to the web of rope draped over the right side of the *Majesty's Pride*. Once on board he reports directly to the *Pride's* captain.

"Captain Ricco. First Lieutenant Nicholas reporting, sir," he salutes his captain. The captain is easily half his age and looks to be a stout fellow.

"Flanagan, show the first lieutenant to the officer's quarters so he can stow his gear. After we will speak frank in my quarters," orders the young captain before he climbs the six-steps leading to the quarterdeck located to the rear of the vessel. Upon stowing his gear Nicholas reports to Captain Ricco in the captain's quarters. Following their first frank and direct discussion they go about the business at hand. As second-in-command he's been handed more duties then he's ever previously had before. With the loading and gathering of supplies and rogue crew members completed they are finally ready to get underway, but with all the stationary time it takes to leave port the ship just won't move quickly enough for Nicholas' anticipation to see the port vanish behind the ship's sails.

3.

Four months pass before they have their first military encounter. The skirmish takes place as the early morning sun rises from its watery bed below the distant horizon of rolling waves. Nicholas nearing the end of his shift upon the quarterdeck makes one last sweep at the surrounding horizon with his spyglass in hand. It is here he spots a Spanish man-o-war laying siege on a British merchant ship to the right of the *Pride* several miles away from their present position. Nicholas quietly calls-to-quarters the *Pride*'s crew, who upon hearing the call race across the main deck to report to their designated positions. In short order everyone is primed and ready for action. Captain Ricco strolls from his quarters and onto the quarterdeck stopping to the right of Nicholas. Before the captain speaks a word he looks over the deck to see everyone is in their assigned position. He looks to all he sees with a slight grin of satisfaction towards the orderly promptness of the *Pride*'s crew and its first lieutenant. This whole self-examination lasts roughly thirty seconds before he turns his attention to First Lieutenant Nicholas.

"What do we have?" he asks as he takes the spyglass from Nicholas's hand to look over to where Nicholas is watching contently.

"It looks to be a Spanish man-o-war attempting to board a British merchant vessel," he replies in a prompt tone of speech.

"What a way to start the day. Mr. Quinn head straight for her, time to earn some of that advance we all received," remarks the captain with a non-vanishing smile on his face. With the order given the captain retracts the spyglass and hands it back to Nicholas. "Lieutenant Mitchell break out the pistols and cutlasses." On this order Captain Ricco turns to the man in command of the marines aboard the *Pride*. In a split-second, the lieutenant has gone from standing at attention directly in front of the quarterdeck to Nicholas seeing only the red of his back as he vanishes below deck heading to the armory of the *Pride*. By the time they near the two mile marker the Spanish ship has not yet noticed their presence. Quietly the captain orders Mr. Quinn to pull alongside them. The captain reasons to have some fun, since the element of surprise is still theirs. He hopes to hook their ship to the Spaniard's so their hull won't take any damage from the Spaniard's superior cannons. Luckily for the captain and crew of the *Pride* Mr. Quinn is a master behind the ship's wheel. On reaching the one hundred and seventy-five foot mark Captain Ricco orders the sails to drop. Giving Mr. Quinn the reduced speed allowing them to be stopped by two dozen triple-talon hooked ropes. With only manageable pull on the ship's main deck walls Mr. Quinn pulls alongside the Spaniards without a scratch to either hull. In a fury of commotion the crew boards the main deck of the Spanish ship with both pistols and cutlasses drawn. The first wave of men disappears within a cloud of bluish gray smoke. Nicholas crosses on to the enemy vessel with the second wave of men. The second wave can't see anything until they come into close contact with the Spanish crew. The Spanish crew acts as though they've been caught up in a sudden and violent tropical storm threatening to destroy them along with the ship. After a short engagement thanks mostly to their element of surprise, the crew of the *Pride* overtake the Spanish vessel with no structural injuries along with a quick capture and surrender from the ship's captain. Upon seeing to the prisoners and other matters needing to be performed upon taking prize of the newly-acquired vessel, the captain meets with his first lieutenant on his return to the *Pride* to hear the report on the details of the capture.

"What are the causalities?" asks Captain Ricco preparing to hear a list.

"Only a few cuts and bruises nothing mortally life threatening," reports Nicholas. "In truth it was a supreme victory, captain."

"What did you find below deck?" probes Ricco

"We found many items to sell in order to fill the men's pockets," returns Nicholas. The captain smiles at this answer and raises his hand to set an encouraging hand on the lieutenant's right shoulder.

"How soon until we can set sail?" inquires the captain lastly.

"Once the prisoners are loaded into the holding cell of the Pride," he answers. A large, but young red-coated marine leads the precession of Spanish prisoners across one of the wood planks connecting the two vessels. The two men watch the beginning portion of the precession before the captain starts to speak again.

"I'm going to have you take command and sail the Spanish vessel to our port in Morton," Captain Ricco explains. "We'll meet up with you there once we've patrolled the rest of the coastline back to the port in Pandoria." Unaware to them one of the Spanish prisoners has concealed a pistol on his person. He's in the second small group crossing onto the *Pride*. On passing by the two officers he takes his chance to pull his concealed pistol firing the round square into Captain Ricco's chest. One of the two marines escorting them pulls his pistol and discharges the metal ball into the Spaniard's skull at point blank range. He falls dead before his wound can run with crimson down the side of his chin.

"DOCTOR!" yells Nicholas as he kneels above his dying captain. Blood spills out from Ricco's mouth.

"It's too late," he says as he struggles to hold onto every last breath. "Take the ships back to port and give this letter to Admiral Aubrey." With his right hand he removes from his inner pocket a letter with an unlabeled red wax seal. On this last action the captain releases his final breath on the ship's main deck. Nicholas looks into the captain's vacant face as the sound of quick-paced footsteps race across the deck. The footsteps belong to the doctor who arrives far too late.

"He's gone," he says to the doctor. Solemnly he walks off the main deck to enter the captain's quarters to fill out a report on the skirmish's outcome in the captain's log after shackling all prisoners and securing them in the brig of the *Majesty's Pride*. The *Pride's* crew holds a ceremony for the late captain as they lay his body to the deep. Later that night Nicholas sitting in his hammock in the captain's quarters is visited by the newly appointed First Lieutenant Stephens.

"Come in. Lieutenant Stephens, what can I do for you at this late hour?" he asks in a non-threatening tone. Since he's unable to sleep he kind of looks forward to this late night intrusion.

"When we arrive in Morton are you going to be given command of the *Majesty's Pride?*" asks the lieutenant.

"Don't know. We'll have to wait and see what Admiral Aubrey decides," remarks Nicholas.

"Are we still on coarse?" asks Nicholas.

"Yes sir, we should reach Morton the day after tomorrow if the sails hold," he answers.

The next two days go by without incident. The Spanish vessel is following the *Pride* at a fair distance. She's commanded by Second Lieutenant Richards and his own handpicked sailing team with exception for a couple of Nicholas's own suggestions. Precisely as Stephens promised they reach Morton in two days. Stephens knocks on the door to the captain's quarters and waits as it's opened from within by Nicholas.

"Stephens, I want you to take charge of escorting the prisoners to the port's jail. I'll call on Admiral Aubrey and deliver the news about the late Captain Ricco. I'll meet you out front of the accountant's office where we can see about an advance on our prize," he orders. Stephens only responds by standing straight and saluting his superior officer. With destinations given Nicholas travels to shore on one of the port's first rowboats.

4.

Nicholas enters the headquarters of Admiral Aubrey and sets eyes on the greenhorn who interrupted the admiral's story all those months ago.

"First Lieutenant Nicholas here to speak with Admiral Aubrey about the logs from the *Majesty's Pride?*" states Nicholas in a formal tone. On this greeting the admiral's aide rises from his chair to cross to the door leading into the admiral's office.

"Well, well, never thought I'd see the day. You look so regal and proper," speaks a voice to Nicholas's immediate right. He turns to see a mid-seasoned captain leaning against the room's wall opposite the front door of the building. It's Captain Colberth, a man who Nicholas has had many an entertaining evening with his wife when the good captain was on deployment, though as far as Nicholas knows he has no idea of this exact fact. "So, you are a first lieutenant on the *Majesty's Pride.* I would like to know how you talked yourself onto that vessel. The captain must've been really dumb or fancied your backside." Upon hearing the ill-tempered talk on the honorably dead Nicholas has to fight from regressing to his old ways of bar fighting, rowdy drinking, and adultery committed onto an endless sea of womanly virtue. Luckily, the greenhorn steps back into the waiting area where each man is viciously trying to stare the other down.

"Admiral Aubrey will see you now First Lieutenant Nicholas," calls the admiral's aide. Nicholas walks through the door held open by the aide in wait for Nicholas. He once more enters the dimly lit office followed by the door shutting in his wake. His eyes take a moment to adjust from the bright daylight to the now lamp-lit room. After a short duration he sees Aubrey sitting behind his oak desk. Nicholas finds it funny to see this site it's as though the admiral hasn't moved since last they met all those months ago.

"Captain Ricco on his dying breath ordered me to give you this, sir," states Nicholas. He pulls the unlabeled red wax-sealed letter from his jacket pocket. Nicholas places the folded letter on the desk in front of Admiral Aubrey. The admiral opens the letter. Once its contents have been read he sets the letter down with the seal broken.

"Captain Ricco died during battle? How did this happen?" asks Aubrey in a solemn tone. Before Nicholas can answer Aubrey speaks again. "I've watched Captain Ricco grow from the main deck of a ship. Never have I been prouder to see a boy rise up in rank. I've known him, since he came aboard his first vessel at the age of seven."

"He died from a Spaniard who concealed a pistol on his person. They were being escorted onto the *Pride* to be secured in the ship's brig. The Spaniard pulled his pistol and shot Captain Ricco in the chest. He died after his final order was given," explains Nicholas solemnly.

"You must have impressed him greatly. He gave you this glowing recommendation," states the grieving admiral. He holds up the now unsealed letter Nicholas gave him moments ago. "With this recommendation I am appointing you captain of the *Majesty's Pride* effective immediately."

"Thank you admiral, you won't regret this," replies Nicholas in the same solemn tone.

"I know I won't," remarks Aubrey. He waves Nicholas to the door. Nicholas understands the order for his wanted departure from the room. "Nicholas. Come back tomorrow for your captaincy papers and tell my aide to cancel the rest of my meetings for the day." Upon exiting the office he searches the room for Captain Colberth, but finds he's already left. Apparently, Colberth's meeting ended when his started, which he finds lucky to not have to interact with him any further.

"Admiral Aubrey asked me to tell you to cancel his appointments for the remainder of the day," he relays to the aide sitting behind his desk.

"He has a day's worth of meetings requiring his attention. I'll speak with him," states the greenhorn. Standing up from his chair he starts to walk from his desk to the admiral's door.

"I wouldn't do that unless you want to lose your head. I just informed him of Captain Ricco's death," explains Nicholas.

"Captain Ricco? Oh God! He was the closest thing to a son the admiral has ever had. I'll cancel the day and if they want to argue they can deal with the admiral themselves," comments the aide.

"I wouldn't want to be them," remarks Nicholas with a chuckle. Turning away from the greenhorn he makes his way out of the admiral's headquarter. Nicholas walks through the port's bustling streets in search of meeting up with Stephens, who's been waiting outside the accountant's office for nearly a quarter of an hour.

"How did it go up there?" he asks as Nicholas comes to a stop beside him.

"I just told the admiral that his sort-of son has been killed. It went about the way you'd expect it to," he replies "It's not really the environment I thought I would be in when I was give my captaincy. The promotion just doesn't seem worth celebrating given the recent loss of Captain Ricco." They enter the office of the accountant to talk him into giving the *Pride*'s crew a two-thirds advance on the sale of the Spaniard's ship and the various cargos she was carrying within. Sometime later, they depart the office with smiles on their faces and a cloth sack filled with prize money in Nicholas's right hand. He hands the sack to Stephens. "Take this back to the ship and divide the money into equal shares amongst the crew and tell them we shall have a two day furlough for them to go ashore, starting this evening.

"Yes, Captain Nicholas," answers Stephens with a salute of his curved right index finger to his eyebrow.

"Belay that. Let's not jump ahead of ourselves. I'm not officially captain yet," he corrects. Stephens lowers his hand back to his side. "However, I do appreciate your enthusiasm Stephens. Now hurry in getting the men their money. They've earned it." With that final farewell Stephens pushes through the midtown crowd heading to the *Pride* to carry out the order given.

Nicholas walks in the opposite direction heading to the supply depot to order the necessary restock on water, gun powder, grog, and fresh food supplies for the *Majesty's Pride*. He thinks about how much he has truly changed in these last few months. The old Nicholas upon hearing his forthcoming promotion would have gone running to the tavern for some pre-celebratory drinks. The new Nicholas, however, is focused on gathering what's needed for the *Pride* and her goodly crew. A solemn grin grows across his face at the complete three-sixty he has undergone. His attention is redirected to the present on realizing it will take an hour to arrive at the supply depot. Due to his misfortune of being marooned here for two months he knows all the back alleyways. In taking this route he should arrive at the depot within fifteen to twenty minutes. Nicholas moves with the slow-moving crowd until he sees the alley's entrance to his right. Quickly ducking down the alley in hopes of no one catching on to what he's doing. The alleys are normally used by locals and drunk sailors to avoid the port authority. The last thing Nicholas wants to do is piss any of them off, because combined they equal two-thirds of the port's population. His mind once again wonders to other matters, while navigating through the decayed darkness of the alley. He's jolted forward by an object making contact with the back of his head. The blow causes him to stumble on the uneven ground of the trash-laden alley. He falls to the ground after taking another hit from behind. This time the object connects with the top of his neck along the base of his skull. His vision grows fuzzy with pain signals sent to his brain. He forces himself to rollover onto his back to see his unknown attacker. Due to his blurred vision all he can see is a darkened silhouette with their long shoulder length hair blowing in the alley's shallow wind in front of a bright white sky. Not until the attacker speaks does he realize who it is.

"You didn't think I'd find out?" yells the attacker. "I know you as a slime of a man, a plague to everyone you're around. We were raised together as young lads. I thought you might have had some sentiment towards me, but you proved your self-arrogance knows no bounds," rants the attacker. Nicholas watches helplessly as the attacker raises a long rectangular object into the white sky above him. The attacker prepares for the final blow. A blow Nicholas is in no fixed state to ward off. He tries to command his body to action, but in mutiny his limbs disobey. Nicholas is only able to raise his left hand up in defense toward the silhouette silently pleading him to stop. This action momentarily calms the attacker's growing tension to strike.

"I know I wronged you greatly. There is a great many things I've done in my past I regret. I know I probably do deserve this, but in these last few months I have changed a great deal. If you do what you're planning you will be no better then I once was. I beg you Captain Colberth do not do what it is you are planning. I won't tell anyone and your honor will be restored," pleads Nicholas. Faint traces of crimson liquid are coughed up and run down the sides of his mouth.

"It truly does sound as though you've changed. If only I didn't know you I might actually have a change of heart. Have no fear you go not alone my wife is already waiting for you in Hell!" says Colberth sending the final blow cracking Nicholas's head. Nicholas lies on the rat-occupied alley floor twitching with the last of the leaking crimson liquid pooling under his fractured skull. Colberth reaches into his captain's jacket and withdraws a pistol. He points the pistol to his right temple and with a click followed by a bang Colberth falls to the side of Nicholas. Colberth's dark crimson mixing with that of his victim's. The shot quickly attracts onlookers who fill this once empty alleyway. With speed the news travels across the port town to the ears of both Admiral Aubrey and First Lieutenant Stephens.

5.

"First Lieutenant Nicholas lived a life on the sea. She was his true love. Many could not understand his tone of attitude so they wrote his expert seamanship off as arrogance. He was a better seaman then most men could ever dream of being. His passing is premature to say the least and though this may come too late. I hope it will show his doubters what kind of man he was capable of being. I feel it's only fitting that his final voyage to sea should be that of a captain," Admiral Aubrey farewells as he hands his aide a sealed envelope. The aide wedges it on top of Nicholas's wooden coffin. "I agree with the others who truly knew him. This is a most fitting burial, one which Nicholas would have preferred." The aide signals to Captain Stephens of *Majesty's Pride* to cast off to end the ceremony. The ship tightens the rope connecting the *Pride* to Nicholas's wooden coffin raft with a single crude makeshift sail located in the raft's center. *Majesty's Pride* departs port with Admiral Aubrey and the others back on shore saluting Captain Nicholas for the first and last time. The *Pride* will pull Nicholas's vessel until they are far out to sea. The rope will be severed and Nicholas' sailing raft will be set free. The miniature vessel will sail away for far adventures many will soon explore and many more having already been sent to explore.

The Creature

In darkness it hid. In darkness it hunted. A monstrous creature too unbelievable to describe though I will try. Try as I will to relay what at present I have witnessed. The shocking horror of an unimaginable thing preying upon London's helpless and discarded. I lived to tell this tale leading to my own survivor's recompense of guilt. In truth, I wish not to speak on it, nor to be made to relive this whole haunting ordeal. Sending shivers down my spine. If in relaying my tale I save, but one life from so excruciating an end. My words will have performed a charitable service. I do hope all who give over the time to these words take my telling as fact. Through my retelling of this tale it most assuredly will sound more like wildly fictitious fiction. As the old saying goes, *truth often times is stranger than fiction.* Heed my words and give prudence to my fears. All future deaths hang off a mourner's tears.

Friday -- last day of the week for business-oriented gentlemen such as myself. I work for a shipping outfit off the London docks. We ship vessels to all outlying parts, the world over. The week had ended with another most profitable increase. What with imports from the colonies, though I do hear a revolt against the crown may well be imminent. If so, at what time this occurs the company will take a brief shortage in income, but little worries. They will simply have to double their focus in the routes heading into the orient. A healthy return they will see from the goods brought in from there too. The highest in-demand market they own, which is not soon to wither.

I'm a single being of comfort, a proclaimed bachelor, no family do I have. My parents long since died leaving me their home. It is a modest twin story place down a street of those living off a moderate income. This fact leaves my taxes and expenses manageable. On Fridays, I take to supper out and spend my evening late upon the local tavern nearest my permanent lodgings. A fine old Irish tavern filled with plenty of evening's entertainment. I may live and be alone, but I'm social amongst friends along with those of a more feminine company. To the latter I have many. This Friday it was late into November with the festive holdings of the season fast approaching. Sometimes, this is the time of year where I do take to wonder if I want more in my life. Then I think of my days spent pursuing my own passions away from work and thusly the feelings pass. This night it was of an extra chill even considering the time of year. I exited from the tavern with comfortable warmth in my belly and a head clouded as to hold my problems at bay for another day. On the whole I felt joyful on the state of my existence in life. The chill on the breeze signaled me to lift my coat's collar. The collar was raised passed my ears, a pleasing feature, which was what led me to purchase this particular article of clothing. What with my office, tavern, and home within walking distance my outerwear's added luxuries toward winter comfort was a most vital selling point. My knee-length wool coat is button fully with collar raised. My scarf secured 'round my neck to shield my throat from the frigid bite of the coming winter frost. As one can tell, like they say, *snug as a bug in a rug.* I made my way down the gaslight-lit cobblestone street where London's thick fog and a dusting of powdery white snow mingles into one. My hands I buried into my coat's lower front pockets to give aid to my at-risk extremities. The night surrounds dark and lifeless in the outlining borders where the gaslight dares not to tread. As though, a thousand horrors wait for the gaslight's illumination to give life onto them. These horrors appear to be in a perpetual state of hibernation, while cloaked in veiled darkness of a most moonless night. This gives little comfort for neither man nor beast who might stumble into their fateful embrace.

I walk my familiar path like I have done for countless Fridays. Only too fitting my path to hell -- my tavern, is set in the direct opposite direction from my path to heaven -- my church. Where I attend mass every Sunday and read from the good book of God's teachings. One's life I've learned is a long series of prolonged pauses followed by labored starts and stops. On this night, my pause, start, and stop were to become all intertwined in a singular instance. I walked uneven in step across the cobblestone through the flickering illuminating bubbles of the gaslight. The bitter cold seemed to harden my joints causing each step on hinged knees to be a new exercise in pain. My neck has all, but receded into my coat and through my lower extremities comes the feeling of the bite from this unnatural night. All within the confines of this exquisitely warm piece of outerwear I am snuggled cozy. No other souls have I seen on my walk back to my lodgings. It's a brisk twenty minute walk through the night's darkness. Supremely focused was I to enter my abode and take my well-deserved rest beside my warming fireplace before I retire to my bed's intimate embrace. I noticed not the added echoes of steps moving within the wake of my own.

A pair of despicable rogues followed behind me from a shadow's gaze. They take to darkened corners in unlit alleyways to wait out a suitable victim. In some small way, suppose, I should feel flattered by their choice landing upon my shrunken brow. More dedicated men to their craft never will they be found. Seeing as how diligent they braced the cold night in order to carry out their forthcoming onslaught. The pair stepped from out of their darkened concealment. At first they move with a timid caution before the pair of men pick up their pace by more than half a step. This increase gave assistance to help shrink the gap between rogues and prey. They fell upon me by the next alley we come to pass. I was blissfully unaware of their descent, due to my own thoughtless distractions. Many times one takes to lose feeling of his natural instincts. There by tossing them into the world to be served up as mutton to the wolves of society.

A swift blow to the back of the head caused me to nearly collapse onto the cobblestone. If it not for these two men taking a hold of me from up under my arms in guidance. They proceed to guide our way down into the darkness of the featureless alleyway. For the first few minutes my mind was floating in a foggy cloud of garbled words and inaudible phrases. The two men rummaged with aggressive hands searching my clothes for any trinkets they could use to collect a few copper coins.

"He has hardly a thing on him. Bollocks!" commented the larger of the two men in an angered tone. "This is the last time I let you pick 'em, Rumley."

"Like your picks have favored any fortune on us," countered the shorter man.

"Oh shut your trap -- before I do it for you," slurred the bigger one. I rocked to and fro from their vigorous search through my pockets. Having pulled out the contents of my last pocket the big man tosses the scattered junk across the alley's floor. "To hell with him cut his throat and let's be off."

"Cut his throat?" questioned Rumley. "But Gregory, you said we were to rob 'em not randomly kill 'em."

"I know what I said," returned Gregory. "Any man not carrying even a fiver doesn't need to waste his breath. He couldn't afford it any-how." Rumley removed a partially rusted blade from out of its sheath hooked onto his belt. The blade was plagued by the dull splotches of red rust, except for the sharp well-kept cutting edge of the blade. The knife's blade looked to be around five inches in length. From the dark-ness and my loss of focus the blade seemed to sway back and forth in the dim light. I assume it's more likely, due to the swaying of my own head. Rumley's face looks with an expression of graveness. It's an expression commonly associated by an unwillingness to step fully into an unwanted commitment. Neither he nor I knew what had be-come of Gregory. Garbled sounds filled our ears calling attention to the sudden abruptness of the big man's apparent absence. The sound was abrupt and seemingly cut short. I felt in my present state, my faculties weren't in any way a thing to be trusted. The man called Rumley spun to his left to look into the vacant darkness of the alley.

Gregory?" called Rumley with an unmeasured degree of nervous apprehension. His attention might have been fixed on the vacant space. However, his long pointed blade was still aiming its stinger on me. Rumley calls his friend again, but with an anxious unease in his words. Turning his attention back to me he poked the blade forward into the air. "What did you do with him? Gregory!" Even in my state I found his questioning absurd. Fear, I reasoned, had taken full control of Rumley's own faculties. Terror had a firm grip on him with unrivaled torment having seeded deep into his mind. His attention shifted back to the void with eyes trying to pierce the veil of black to secure any sign of where Gregory had fled. A shape, I think I saw in the black void, but tricks of the mind do still plague my thoughts from this moment in my memories. A strong beating taken will alter ones past recollection of what was or what the mind believed it had at one time seen. On what happened next has been foremost on my mind and in debate ever since I stumbled on shaky legs out of that alley on that particular night ending with the transfer from night to day. Like a drunkard, I stumbled onto the street between the once lit gaslights by shaky feet I traversed. The few fellow travelers I had encountered along the way did little to aid my physical plight. Except granting on me a wide berth. From shaky stance I did my best, but by a throbbing pulse my limbs did eventually abandon me. So collapsed had I and with luck to avoid the street's hoof-led carriages and hansoms occupied by early morning commuters. To sleep I fell and had not woke before a swift kick did muster me to wake. From the foot words seemed to jester forth. My eyes hung heavy from my inner eye's ache -- a throbbing primer from a primal rage. The beating was far greater than I had previous realized. Looking up by an encouraged series of groans I did see for the first time the man standing above me. My eyes rested on a bobby, who stood looking at me. I could tell he was watching my disoriented mobility along with the fog still occupying my head from the beating I had so shortly endured.

"Been drinking have we?" asked the policeman in a rhetorical tone. "Looks like you bite off a bit more than you could chew. Got your block knocked 'round? Come with me -- your sort is not welcomed amongst civilized folk such as there are here." He set a firm hand on the back of my upper arm and led me down the cobble street. By the sheer thickness of the fog clouding my mind I could not tell in what direction we did head. Only I'm sure a station was along the path's conclusion.

By Monday morning I was out of lock up and thrown back on the street. The tank, a not-so-clever name for a specific cell held for drunken vagrants to sleep one off. A stiff fifty pound fine was placed on my shoulders. An easy enough sum to muster come my next pay packet. In three day old clothes I proceeded to my home to change and straighten myself up. A fright would be had if I returned to my place of employment as I currently was.

Once through the door my garb was stripped away until I stood in the buff. I moved through my flat to the wash basin before heading to the bathtub filled with an hour's worth of warmed water. The warm water felt good on my sore muscles and bruises I sustained from the attempted robbery days prior. Over my incarceration I had plenty of time to replay the night's events over in my head several times. I had spoken with a policeman to give a detailed account of the robbery and what followed. I figure it was easier for them to chock it up to a drunkard's hallucination than a truthful retelling of actual events. Further -- of what proof did I have? Even still, I scarcely believed what my own eyes saw firsthand. Either what I saw is what I saw, or had my brain given over to the thrashing set I took by the hands of those two scoundrels? Had those two truly been sent to their deaths or simply vanish into the darkness? For if I can't even give over to my own decision to what hope do I give toward another believing me? These thoughts gave over adding more turmoil during my incarceration.

It's the thought on Rumley, which is where my mind kept returning. What I saw or rather what I think I saw. If true, fills my soul with fearful dread. Fear can drive a man to flee from its source or chase headlong after it to prove to himself if what he saw was truly what he saw. On this latter I have given choice, because I must first prove to myself before I can hope to prove onto another. All I centered on was Rumley, the poor chap. I still feel he had simply fallen in with the wrong sort of blokes. I should tell of what I saw though I know you won't believe me. Why would anyone believe the words of a madman? Rumley stood over me like I previously stated. His stare was fixed onto the darkness with his sharp-edged blade trained on me.

"Gregory?" he called into the void with his words seemingly soaked in fear. His voice sounded like that of childish fear from a young boy screaming out into the night in dread of the monsters lurking beneath his bed. His gaze stayed on the darkness with every ounce of his being trying to penetrate the void with his dim inner light. Hoping to see his companion of ill-intent standing in wait, unharmed. This however does not come to pass. Looking back is the dark void filled with every man's fear -- the fear of the unknown.

My fear rose from what I saw, but to which, Rumley saw not. It seemed to slither, or rather grow along the muck-filled ground, outstretching from the void moving in a slanky motion much like a serpent. The limbed mass looked to resemble a tentacle formed from out of the darkness of the void. The limb grows both in thickness and distance while curling behind Rumley. I tried to speak. To warm him, but the words seemed to elude me. Either by my own fear or by the beating I previously undertook, from which truth I'm not sure. All I know is I sat there and witnessed the horror unfold.

The black limb rose behind Rumley who remained unaware. When he learned of the tentacle it became too late for any resistance. The tentacle wrapped over his back and down across his torso. The limb locked him into a death grip. This next sight will haunt me for the rest of my natural born days, even if I live to a hundred and twelve. The limb raised Rumley from off the ground like one pulls a carrot from the earth. In a state of shock Rumley was held up with his feet dangling and his arms hanging by his side, outstretched. It was almost as if it was a sign of his unspoken surrender. His back was facing me and so I could not read his face, but it could have been no other expression than that of sheer terror. With its prey held helpless the long tentacle like limb slowly retracted into the concealment of the darkness consuming the alley's black void. I hear not a sound as Rumley's body crosses the void's border causing my eyes to witness the illusion of the black absorbing him. Rumley is gone. Though my still sluggish sight tried, I could not find a single sign of Rumley, nor of the limb returning for me. Silence filled the alleyway. This form of silence seemed to grown all the more eerie by the unknown creature taking refuge within the black.

The only sign of Rumley to escape was to hear a short cry directly followed by what I can only describe as a bone-crunching sound. Just as swiftly the barrage of more unending silence returned to my ears. From my seated position I stayed, not moving. Fear had taken its hold upon me rendering my body to the possession of full paralysis. Sat did I, frozen until the bluish hue of pre-dawn's light pushed the blackness of the alley into its daily seclusion. This washing illumination seemingly freed me from this horrid night of horrors. By the departure of the darkness I rose from my seated position. With all haste I made my way out of that cursed alley. As I departed I kept an ever watchful glance behind me. Not sure if I was truly in the clear or if the thing consumed in darkness was merely toying with me.

On making my final exit from the alley and into the wide open space of the cobblestone street I was finally able to breathe a lung-filled sigh of relief. Attempted did I to walk back on shaky legs to my flat, which proved to be a fruitless endeavor. This is where I previously discussed of my sudden rest upon the cobblestone and to the policeman's following wake up call. From here, I will skip back before I regressed to explain as to my witnessed observation of Rumley's fate.

Following my bath as previously stated, I sat in my favorite reading chair and looked to my fireplace's dancing flames. My thoughts gave over thinking in depth on my most horrifying of nights. Further I had given to reason upon my own senses, to have been duped by a vividly detailed drunken hallucination brought on by too much ill-stored spirits. Coming to this self-conclusion I was free to return to my daily life without as much as a tremor of doubt. For the situation proposed beyond the obvious answer of too much drink was far too crazy to possibly be true. Yet, in the back of my mind it did linger. These crazy events preceded picking away at my arguing reason. The hours passed to days, days to weeks, and still this clawing unreasonable thought remained. I do believe as the days rolled on my mind's thoughts had given to falter. I feel it was here where my reason breeched the insanity. To bring thought around to justify such thought as truth. Oh how I beseech you, dear reader, give belief to my proclamation. I tried, oh, how I tried to fight it. For many days I tried in a desperate measure to return to my lack luster days of yore. This endeavor was fruitless, because every dark crevice and alleyway filled me with unspoken fright. As time persisted I knew what I must do to settle these fears. To give even the slightest return to normalcy.

Two days time after obtaining certain supplies. I departed my flat at the dusk of day. While others ventured home to rest their weary bones before slumber took hold. I wandered the darkened alleys and slumming side streets. I found myself on the hunt. For what creature I most surely know not. When we two meet I will know it. I walked, walked countless miles over black slime-covered passageways where all manners of trash be laid. By the greeting light on the eve of a new day's sun I took my leave. To my flat I dragged my wayward soul to give over to rest -- in wait for the 'morrow's night. On this final thought I gave to utterance as my head set to pillow. This course will be made true . . . or by week's end I shall be rightly consumed by madness, too far gone to ever return.

Five days hence my exploratory venture began with nothing to show, but my maddening resolve to lunacy. All resemblance toward my past existence has faded into the void of obsession. Now finding the creature is not merely a want, but a necessity. Of what I hope to gain by its discovery passed the point of piecing together my fractured sanity, I know not.

This night like the past nights before it, I disembark at dusk to make my way into the dim or unlit passageways lying between the full-sized cobblestone streets of London. With each passage I remove myself from that of which all Londoners see. Instead I stepped within the shadows of the city's underbelly. I walk amongst the desperate and depraved. For many it is a means for survival, but for a select few it's an enticing depravity there is no returning from. The true purpose of throwing my own self into this world is due to the singular purpose -- that and nothing more. In, around, and through these dark passageways I navigate. Almost blending into this shadowy world becoming one with nothing and yet I feel whole when I'm here. It is a strange feeling for one to simultaneously feel lost and found in the same moment.

On this very night my luck did change. How I wish it had not come to pass for it still weighs heavy on my heart. In the world of shadow I did find him. This haunted man plagued by his own growing shadow, whose despair led his path to interweave within my own. Though to tell his tale like my own, I wish I had not to embark down this darkly-lit road. His tale takes on a far greater sadness. I must move ahead for fear and procrastination does his tale wrong. As I said on this night our paths did meet.

I embarked down one of the lengthier alleyways I saw a fellow stranger moving my way, but from the opposite side of the alley. His clothes were stained or to give better description would be to say *"filthy"*. If I be honest my own looks much the same. He looks to also be of a set purpose, as do I. Our eyes met and on this one glance we knew the other's truth. He's seen it too. The closer we came to one another, the slower our pace became. Finally, we stopped on merging in the alley's center.

"My name is Thomas," says the new stranger. His voice seemed to slip, like he had a nervous tick. "You have seen it too?" Without an utterance of a word I nodded with a solemn intensity. Thomas broke down, falling to his knees with his sobs seeming to be equal parts surreal and therapeutic. A further few minutes pass before he manages to retake control of himself. He rose from off his knees, while he wiped his eyes. "I beg apologies, stranger. Too long have I been on my own with this horror. None would take to believe me. To myself I have kept it these last four weeks." We agreed to join up, to work in congress, to find and stop this strange creature of darkness. He had not found it since his first encounter. For all this time he, like me, has not been able to find one sign of the creature.

The day grows near -- night has begun its retreat as will the creature. We headed to take in some coffee, and if not, tea would have to mend us. The day climbed tightly on nine before we did part ways to our restful retreats. However we did agree to meet right where we separated. With nods of farewell we did each take to flight. On the whole trip back to my flat I felt a sense of approval, for I was not alone in my experience. Another had saw, heard, and felt what I had. I was overjoyed. Ever since I saw what I saw, I regularly gave to question my own sanity. Though, looking back I gave no thought as to Thomas's own state of mind, because it gave proof to my cause. Guess in its way it proved my own sanity and within it my self-preservation was in full bloom.

The next evening just after the sun fell behind London's cityscape we met back where we had last departed from one another's company earlier that day. After a time of discussion we entered the seedy entrance to the winding corridors, which were the alleyways flowing between the roadways of London town. Together we make our way down the long labored path of lunacy. We grew to quiet discussion over our lives prior to our horrifying discovery, which lead to where we now find ourselves frequently patrolling these passages of claustrophobic darkness. I recall Thomas speaking of his life prior, spoken like one does on telling a most lucid dream. It's a dream to question one's grip on the truer of two realities. My tale had in a way much of the same tone. Except for my yearning to find a way back to those days of normalcy. As I think back on that conversation I do recall Thomas not expressing this same wanted call back. He was much the reverse. This thing -- this creature of darkness seemed to have become a calling to him. A life's pursuit so to speak was the feeling I find looking back. If I had at the time picked up on this warning. Perhaps, what transpired later that night might not have rendered such a level of shock as it did.

Moving on, the stroke of two chimed with still no sign or hint to the creature's presence. We had made our way from one side and we were over halfway back on our return pilgrimage. It struck upon me to question as to how we could attract the creature into revealing itself. The question was being posed toward finding forthcoming solutions or possible causes as to what attracted the creature in the first place. I further gave question to Thomas on the surrounding circumstances leading to his fateful meeting with the creature. He gave a moment's thought for a time before speaking his articulated answer. Thomas's face shifts to one of sudden abrupt self-realization.

"It is the violence," Thomas says in a tone of realization. "The violence beacons the creature forth. If we wish to find it we must give over to becoming those we saw it take." Thomas races down the alleyway in a sudden burst of energy with my lit lantern in hand and a maddened smile held firm on his face. From the spilt second look from him I knew no good would come from this. I tried in vain to keep up with him, but being as he had held my lantern I was left to hobble through the alley in a blinded pursuit. The dancing flicker of light did wander to keep a target set on him until around a newly arrived corner in the alley the light faded to darkness. Fearing for any unsuspecting person he was to come across I tried in desperate depravity to move with all the haste I could manage. After a time I found myself exiting back onto the conjoining cobblestone street we had previously entered a short time ago. I stood frozen in step not sure as to what direction Thomas had dashed through. My choice was made for me on hearing angered speech followed by a fearful cry and ending in a loud hard smack from the entrance to the alley on the other side of the cobblestone. With more stable legs than I know why I descended the dark abyss filling the alley.

On entering the alley my senses seemed to heighten though my sight was greatly reduced to nothing. My hearing seemed to grow beyond their normal abilities. From my crunching steps and the slimy suction of whatever grime I was standing on I could hear it all individually. From outside of my immediate area I could hear the unknown woman's silent sobs echoing down the unlit corridor. A mumbled hate-filled voice I could also hear coming from who I can only assume was Thomas. My courage was locked to the sticking point I braved my way through the darkness with only my hands to truly guide me along the alley's wall. Otherwise I would have run face first right into them. My fingers ran along the walls of bricks, cold and at times taken over by a thin sheet of ice. From here I hear her cries of fear mixing with his words of anger. Moving forward I push ahead in search of the noises' source. Making a turn I spot the dancing flicker of flame standing within this suffocating fog of darkness. The flickering light guides me to and vanishes behind another turn in the corridor of utter darkness. Making the turn I come to see the hovering flame had stopped off in the near distance. This is where I first see them. With each of them focusing on themselves and the other. This attention rendered me a nonentity in their situation. With a hollow resolve I stand tall, now is my time to take my heroic mark.

On my first step I slip to fall face first to the ground. The pair took no notice, oblivious, so nestled in their own world of pain and anger. It is here where it comes. Simultaneously coming from and being of the alley's darkness. I watch in shocked terror as the creature appeared from behind Thomas with a silent grace. The tentacle wafted in the torchlight like a vapor mist of smoke wrapping around his leg, but before I could open my mouth to warn him. Thomas falls to the wet mucky ground with a thud. This is the time he notices me. His eyes stare straight at me filled by a blank expression of fear. Right before he is plunged into the dark form beneath the creature. I rose to my feet with every intention to charge forth with whatever gusto I could find to help fight off this living nightmare. Yet again froze I did, but stared deeply into the darkened void. The blackness rolled and seemed to writhe in on itself. In the dark the movement seemed to stop. This is when it moved toward me. One by one I looked into what I can only describe as round bulbous suction cup looking appendages attacked to the smoky black tentacle. They seem fixed on me with a dedication of purpose. I felt if ever I felt my time had come this was it. The tentacle surrounded me in this darkness and from out of its seething, churning liquid smoke of form it came. Never will I forget, out of its dark writhing appendage I was approaching something more -- something firmer than its limb. I knew not the creature's anatomy. What it should or could have been. Was it its head, stomach, elbow -- honestly I knew not. Little difference would it really matter if I knew. From this solid form the darkness of the creature split to show an oval-shaped eye nearly the size of my chest. Yellow was it in color with twin slits of red, I can only reason these slits to being the creature's pupils. The eye looked into me, or at least it seemed to look into me. The eye opened wide and stared for a prolonged duration studying me with an honest look into my body's character. Below the elongated eye something more protruded toward me out of the darkness. It was a form made of hardened black stone, cone-shaped. The hardened shape split in two to reveal what has been kept hidden beneath. The cone-shaped appendage appears to be the creature's beak. On this harden shell separating into two it reveals several rows of razor-sharp teeth circling the beak's interior. On this sight a calming fear takes hold of me. My moment of departure is at hand. This obsessing observation has brought me to my end, here and now. I stood my ground in acceptance of my coming fate, my time to die. Fear gripped my body firm to this rooted place. My only peace is in knowing I will soon suffer no more. I close my eyes on seeing its slithering tentacle enclose around me. Outwardly, I feel waiting for the slimed appendage to pull me into its razor-edged teeth. I exhale my held breath in hope the lack of oxygen will subdue my momentary scream. Anticipation grips me, choking me to the core. This unwavering angst sends my nerves into a spasm of convolution. I tense on hearing the tentacle move along the mucky ground around me. Any second I will cease to be in existence. I push through these emotionally-sound thoughts only to be passed over onto the other side assaulted by abrupt absolute silence. This sudden rapture gave onto me its own form of terror. With a readied heart I opened my eyes. Not sure of the sight I was to behold. Like a veil being lifted, my eyes opened to see the distinct lantern still feeding its dancing flame within its glass cage. The woman lies where she was being assaulted by Thomas. Her sobs have ceased to flow leaving only the casual drip of the collected droplets of moisture to smack into the puddles of muck decorating the alley floor. No more was the creature surrounding me, studying me with its measuring eye. Not wanting was I found and so left to ripen to maturity further down the walk of life. With a swivel of my head to make certain the creature had vanished I broke from my previous hold. I make my way to the young woman lying motionless on the mucky ground. I checked her vitals to find she lives still. Scooping her into my arms I take her back to my flat to rest awhile in hopes to help clear away her fear and shock. By mid-morning I awoke in my favorite reading chair to find the bed where she rested vacant. To have made her escape tells me of her healthy demeanor.

All of the days and most of the following weeks I waited on the authorities to bust down my door to drag me off to jail. Never did they come and no one of any other ilk did pay me or my flat homage. On these weeks passing I am of the honest belief, good and plenty, I am in the clear. From every following night since that night in the darkness where finite judgment dispensed fate's resolute rewards. My mind has been unable to venture away from those events. To move forward I can't, and yet, by sparing my life I feel the need to -- I must. Otherwise, to what point was my mercy granted? May my thoughts be saved by relieving these memories onto the page and with these harden proofs telling this tale of my experience may I be reborn anew. The creature looks deep into one's soul determining who it will take and who it will spare. By my own events it has an attraction to torment. Tormentors are warned a warning to alter one's ways and breach onto a new path before it comes for you. In darkness you'll hide. In darkness it hunts.

This monstrous creature too unbelievable to describe though I'm sure there are those who have tried.

The narrator of this strange other-worldly tale sits across from two fine suited gentlemen whom he invited to meet. The back corner table is stationed inside this crude hovel of this dive bar masquerading as a tavern. This lie made evident by the hanging sign above the front door. The man has seen better days with his weakened shell shaking with abruptly sudden jitters of worn nerve. The two men across from him are men of distinction within these London streets. Inspectors Cody and McIntire of Scotland Yard, known in the lower bowels of London for bringing down a murderous nest of would-be witches and some monstrous creatures plaguing the depths of the Jewish quarter. He knew if anyone would listen and take a chance to believe his story it would be these two men.

"Well now, that was quite a harrowing tale you told," remarks Inspector Cody, the younger inspector with three vertical one-inch scarred scratches. "You are really lucky to be alive, sir." Inspector McIntire, the portly inspector sitting to Cody's left gives an agreeing nod with a face filled by his trademark stoically emotionless expression.

"Do you know what it was?" asks the nerve-shaken man. Cody thinks a brief moment before shaking his head confidently.

"Not come across such a thing in my encounters," he answers. "I will have to give the matter some consideration in order to find out its truth."

"How do you hope to do that?" he questions further.

"I have my sources to lean on," Cody returns with a polite grin. The man gives a returning smile and a hopeful nod.

"Thank you," he begins. "You don't know the relief I feel on having told my strange story to someone who would not simply take to openly mock me." Both men sitting across from him give knowing nods with telling looks, which seem to say *we've been there a time or two.*

"We thank you for telling us your terrifying ordeal," farewells the inspector. The nervous man slides from out of the booth walking with a slight limp through the main floors collection of tables and chairs until he exits through the establishment's front doorway. The portly inspector slides out of the bench seat neighbored beside his partner. Spinning around the end of the table he takes to slide onto the seat opposite from his fellow inspector. He looks to the empty door releasing a heavy sigh accompanying his discriminating glance. The slim inspector looks to his fellow companion with a smile holding back his knowing chuckle. "What is with the long face, Albert?" McIntire looks to his friend with a skeptical expression. A look Cody has grown use to seeing every time he tells his half-baked theories to whatever case they are actively pursuing.

"Mathew do you really believe his ravings?" asks McIntire. "About an all consuming blackness living in the shadows feasting on those planning to commit acts of ill-intent onto others?"

"Why not?" poses Cody accompanied by his own stoic expression.

"I mean," starts McIntire. "You saw him. The guy was not right in the head probably suffering a bad spell from chasing the dragon." Cody slightly nods his head slow and in short strokes.

"True. He could be," Cody agrees.

"But . . ." McIntire surrenders with a sunken dip to his chin. He knows full well Cody will not simply leave this to lie. Cody's smile shows for a brief second.

"But . . . it's not too much trouble to take a short amount of time to inquire about any odd disappearances in relation to London's alleyways," Cody explains, finishing the sentence his partner started. McIntire shakes his head knowing any further arguments will fall on deaf ears. In the end after all his day's bluster they will inevitably taxi down this line of questioning just to kick the bucket and see how far down the rabbit hole they can fall.

Author's Note

Well, I hope you enjoyed this scattered collection of tales. I find short story collections allow every reader to find at least one story they truly enjoy. For instance, my mother is quite partial to **Redcap Asylum**, My wife prefers **Planet of Hopeful Madness** (although it involves me burning our kids alive??). My preferred favorite is **The Damned Rain**, due to the concept I've tried to express for years until I wrote this story in nearly one complete sitting. I love the concept of the selfish having to spend the rest of eternity giving life to -- well, life. That thought derived from one day sitting on the porch watching the rain pour down, it is true, ideas can come from anywhere.

I want to add, this is a second REVISED edition of at the Dusk of Madness. Though I corrected many grammatical errors within the stories and rewrote many sentences to give it my style of flow. I did not touch the stories themselves. They are as they were when I first began the revision. Though to me these stories are each perfect in their own way and no need to change the source. For me this revision was a stroll down memory lane meeting old friends in places and times that had partially faded from my mind over the last 13 years.

I'm sure now that you're done reading this collection you are ready to close this book and decide which adventure you should undertake next from your personal bookshelves. For that matter I should go and work on my next tale so at some point we'll meet again. Until then -- goodbye, JB.

For more information on Joshua Bunnell and Devil's Play Publishing books, merchandise, events or to send a message.

go to :
www.devilsplaypublishing.com
Follow on Facebook
JBunnell Fiction